Hardy's hand streaked to his gun. He was fast as lightning, they had always told him that, and now his gun was out of its holster, coming up, he was moving fine, as he always did before the kill, his eye on Slocum's heart. He was fast...

And that was his last thought as Slocum's bullet exploded in his brain.

OTHER BOOKS BY JAKE LOGAN

JAKE LOGAN

SLOCUM'S CRIME

BERKLEY BOOKS, NEW YORK

SLOCUM'S CRIME

A Berkley Book/published by arrangement with
the author

PRINTING HISTORY
Berkley edition/January 1985

ISBN: 0-425-07460-9

A BERKLEY BOOK ® TM 757,375
Berkley Books are published by The Berkley Publishing Group,
200 Madison Avenue, New York, N.Y. 10016.
The name "BERKLEY" and the stylized "B" with design are trademarks
belonging to Berkley Publishing Corporation.

PRINTED IN THE UNITED STATES OF AMERICA

SLOCUM'S CRIME

1

She lit the lamp with a lucifer. It threw a low yellow
glow over the room, and she said, "Take some whiskey, John Slocum." She calmly pulled her red dress
over her head and, bold as brass, added, "Then you
can take me."

It wasn't much of a house that Maisie had brought
him to, just clapboard over logs roughly put together.
There was a low wooden bed, two chairs, a scarred
oak table, and on it two tin cups and a whiskey bottle.

Slocum stared at the saucy lady, then grinned. The
grin looked good on his strong, tanned face with its
piercing green eyes. His lean, powerful body moved
with catlike grace to the table and he poured the whiskey.

Just twenty minutes ago, in Reilly's Saloon and
Dance Hall, she'd swaggered up and brashly asked

him to dance. And, after ten minutes of snuggling tight against him on the dance floor, she asked if he'd like a party. She was one sexy filly, with more curves than the trail into Abilene. The flesh of her breasts pushed hard against her red dress, and the dark eyes of her pretty face glinted with hidden fire.

He'd been on the trail, riding hard for days, trying to get the taste of Abilene out of his system, and the craving of his flesh was strong. Maisie looked just right, a bit on the meaty side, but he liked that.

She didn't waste time. She seemed to be in a hurry. She brought him to this house, and there she was, peeling her clothes like she couldn't wait for the games to start. She had plump white breasts, sexy hips, a nice pair of legs, and looked tempting in the glow of the lamp. His flesh began to tingle. He gulped some whiskey and moved to her. She put her mouth up and gave him a scorcher of a kiss.

"What are you waiting for, Slocum?" she demanded. "Get your duds off. How'm I goin' to get to that man-sized thing of yours?"

Slocum grinned: a low, lusty, big-breasted woman, just what his body craved. He peeled his buckskins, flung them on the chair. Then, naked as a plucked rooster, he came toward her, his male flesh ready for a hard game of fun.

Her eyes went big at the sight of him, and she slipped to her knees just as the door crashed open and two big men rushed in with drawn Colts.

Slocum froze; he was too far from his own gun, something he rarely let happen, and he was naked, about as vulnerable as a man could be. One of the men, the bigger one, with a short, scraggy red beard and hard brown eyes, held his gun steady on Slocum, then grinned coldly.

"Well, lookit John Slocum, like a bull in heat. Ain't it a shame to break in at a time like this?" He turned to Maisie, nodded. "Okay, you can get into your clothes and clear out, pronto." Maisie shrugged, threw on her clothes with never a glance at Slocum, and went out the door fast.

The bitch set me up, Slocum thought.

He stared at the men; he didn't know them, though it hit him that he could have known someone like them. They had to be brothers, both red-headed with broad, fight-scarred faces, short red beards, hard mouths, and stocky bodies. A knife scar decorated the cheek of the bigger man.

Slocum spoke politely to him. "Do you mind if I put my clothes on, mister?"

"Call me Red. And I do mind." He turned. "Clem!" Clem scooped up Slocum's clothes and took them out the door. Red smiled grimly. "That's to let you know you're not going anywhere."

Slocum stared hard. "What's this about? I don't remember meeting you or doing you a mischief."

Red's mouth tightened and anger flashed in his yellow-brown eyes. "Oh, you didn't do nothin' to me, but you did plenty. Still, I'm going to prove I got no hard feelings. Goin' to let you go on with your li'l party." He stopped, as if tickled by his thoughts. Clem came back into the room, his yellow eyes staring balefully at Slocum.

"What do you mean?" Slocum asked.

Red slumped on the chair, his gun pointing. "Oh, not with Maisie. A nicer filly, much nicer. Fact is,

Slocum, she's goin' to knock your blasted eyes out. Most beautiful girl you ever saw."

Slocum grimaced. This mangy dog had to feed on loco weed. He didn't make sense. But he *did* look familiar. Was it someone from back in Calhoun County?

Red grinned. "I can see you don't believe me. Well, it's true. We just hate to interrupt your fun, so we're goin' to swap Maisie for a sweet young filly. That's it. She's all yours. No strings."

He paused and his eyes gleamed with malice. "She's a virgin—a blushin' virgin. Never had a man. No, never. Might be because she's a bit young. But you don't mind that. How do you like it, Slocum?"

"Don't like it." Slocum's mouth was hard. "And I won't do it."

"You'll do it," Red said confidently, and he grinned at Clem. Then he called sharply, "Jessie."

The door was kicked open and a hulking, black-haired cowboy came in pulling a young girl wrapped in a yellow blanket. There was a frozen moment, then he rudely jerked the blanket off, leaving her standing still. She was wearing only a chemise. She looked pale and frightened, but made no effort to run, as if she knew it would be useless. She just stood there, her body quivering.

To Slocum she looked like a young fawn, delicate, graceful, her body white, beautifully shaped. Her breasts were young, pointed, and he figured she couldn't be more than seventeen. The sight of Slocum in his skin put the devil's fear in her, and she trembled and turned away.

Slocum's voice was hard. "There's no way I'm going to touch this kid, Red. You can torture me, break my bones, but I'm not going to do it."

Red's yellow-brown eyes filled slowly with rage. He cocked his Colt, put the cold barrel against Slocum's head. "I'd just as soon you didn't do it," he said hoarsely. "It's all I need to blast your brains out for what you did last week to Seth Dalton."

Now it all came together for Slocum: the card game in Abilene where a young gunslinger, drunk and stupid, named Dalton, who didn't like losing, had accused Slocum of cheating and pulled his gun. Slocum of course had had to shoot.

So these were his kin, two brothers, and probably a cousin, out to avenge him. But what strange revenge was this, serving him a young virgin scared out of her wits?

"What's it to be? Do I blow your head off or do you take this girl?" Red's voice rasped.

From the glare in those yellow-brown eyes, Slocum felt he was an instant away from having his brains plastered on the walls. He had to stall; he needed time. "I'll do it," he said.

Red shook himself like a dog, as if trying to get hold of his rage. "Betcha ass you'll do it." He brought the gun down.

"May I ask, Red," Slocum said mildly, "why you're so good to me?"

Red's mouth twisted with cruel amusement. He glanced at Clem and Jessie and their grins, too, were vicious. "Call it charity," he said. "Like the Good Book says, we reward evil with good. Now—" he stood up—"you got ten minutes. And I want to see blood," he growled. "Maidenhood blood, you understand. So, knowing how shy you lovers are, we'll leave you alone."

Jessie shuffled his feet. "Red, why do we hafta leave? We got business to take care of, money business, and we're in a hurry. Let's stay and rush it, watch the fun."

"Yeah," grunted Clem. "Let's watch this hyena tear her apart."

Red stared at Jessie coldly. "You talk too much. I done tole you the way it's gonna be. Now get the hell out."

He turned to Slocum. "I wanta see blood. We'll be on the other side of that door." He led the way and they tramped out, all grinning hideously.

The girl looked sideways at his male body and shivered. She had a sweet face with full lips, light blue eyes, rich, glowing brown hair. She'd been through hell, he figured, and he didn't aim to add to her troubles.

"What's your name?" he asked.

Her voice quavered, "Charity O'Rourke."

Charity! He shook his head, remembering Red's remark about charity—a devilish pun.

"Why do you suppose they want to do this?" he asked.

She shook her head and her blue eyes blinked; she just looked frightened. Then she gazed at the door as if she yearned to go through it, away from her tormentors. What had been done to get her here? Did they beat her, threaten her? Maisie had left his flesh crawling with lust, but the last thing he wanted was to mix with this virgin filly, half-frightened out of her wits.

"We won't do a thing," he said. "Don't worry."

She turned slowly to look at him, almost astonished.

"What?"

He smiled. "I don't want to hurt you. To hell with them."

She took a deep breath. She seemed calmer. "What's your name?"

"Slocum, John Slocum." A fawn, soft, feminine, he thought.

"Mr. Slocum, these men are rotten dogs . . . worse. They'll kill you."

Slocum's voice was gentle. "I'll take my chances." But his chances, he knew, weren't good. He'd killed their brother, and they weren't the kind of men who'd bypass payment. They were gunslingers, and talked about money. Though why they were forcing him into this act seemed crazy.

She shook her head. "Red Dalton is a mad dog. He'll kill you," she repeated.

He stared at her. She was beautiful, untouched, and though she tried to hide it, terrified. What did she fear most, Slocum or the sex? It didn't matter. He couldn't go through with it.

He shook his head. "Maybe they won't."

But the insane rage that he'd seen blaze in Red Dalton's eyes told him otherwise.

Again Charity seemed astonished, and calmer. Clearly, she had expected him to grab her and spear her on the spot, and his gentleness was giving her a lot of different thoughts.

She bit her lip nervously. "I don't want you to die because of me."

Frankly, he shared that view, but he couldn't figure out anything. If only he had a gun. It was all hopeless. "Mr. Slocum," she said, "I'm afraid we have no choice. They'll kill you, and I won't escape what they'll do afterwards."

He took a deep breath. Damn, that was true. Men

like them would not only blow his brains out, but they'd rip her apart . . . all of them. They'd gone too far. Just grabbing her was enough to get a posse on their trail.

She'd been watching his face, trying to read his thoughts. "We have no choice," she said again.

Slocum rubbed his chin. "They want blood. Maybe I could cut my arm and give them blood."

She smiled faintly. "And if that doesn't work? You'll be dead, and I might as well be."

It was true. He sighed. For the moment he was helpless. They had three guns. He didn't have a stitch on him. And Red seemed cut from the same cloth as his brother Seth, who wanted to shoot first and ask later. They were a gang of black-hearted hyenas. What the hell did Red Dalton have up his sleeve? Why did he bring in this virgin filly for sacrifice? No way yet of figuring it. But one thing was sure, he'd get a bullet if nothing happened in this room. And time was running out fast. What must be must be, Slocum thought.

Charity bit her lip. "I'm sorry. I'm scared. I'm new at this. But we must go ahead." She hesitated, a bit trembly, her eyes avoiding his maleness. It had to be a fearful thing to her, at least now. Later it would be different.

"You'll have to tell me what to do," she said.

He took a breath. "Miss Charity, this won't be rape, just a friendly get-together."

She stared at him, trying to understand, then a small smile twisted her full lips. She lifted her chemise slowly and Slocum felt a shock as her white nude body slowly appeared. She was built like a statue of Diana he'd once seen in a book. White smooth flesh all put together perfectly, the breasts pointed with pink tips, the belly flat, the thighs finely moulded, and between them a light brown fuzz that couldn't conceal the pouting lips. She looked virginal all right, a body untouched, unawakened, yet ready to come alive, maybe ready to burn with the passions that were planted in her flesh by nature, waiting for someone to start the fire.

He felt a sudden surge of desire, and his flesh seethed and hardened.

The sight of it made her eyes go saucer-wide, and in them he could see shyness, timidity, curiosity, and, strangely enough, a touch of desire. He told himself to go slow, very slow, or everything would spoil. He waited, smiling at her, motioning with his hand that she come to him. Better she should move at her own pace. She stood still, rooted, two spots burning in her cheeks. He waited.

Then she moved to him slowly, and paused. He took a step, held her head in his hands, put his lips on hers, a gentle kiss. Her lips were full, soft, and tasted like fresh flowers. He kissed her again, then put his arms about her. She shivered. He let her get used to the closeness, moved still closer. And the feel of her flesh was pure velvet. He brought his body near hers, then, as if something happened inside her, she lifted her head, her eyes closed, her mouth ready. He kissed her again. She pressed her body to his. Her breathing had quickened, her face was flushed. He brought his hand to her breasts, caressed them gently, again and again, touching the tips, then bent to put his tongue to the pink nipples. She stood tight and taut, and it was clear magic things were going on inside her. His hands began to caress her body, her hips, her buttocks. She was beautifully shaped.

His hand moved between her thighs over the fuzz. His finger entered the crease. She was tight, impossibly tight, but there was wetness. He stroked the crease and her body went limp; she seemed to be hypnotized.

He kept stroking, always gently, then lifted her and carried her to the bed. She lay like a white statue, waiting.

He put his maleness against the opening and pushed, went in, felt her warmth and wetness. His instinct to drive in was overwhelming, but he kept control, waited, pushed further. Her thighs widened automatically, as if she was under nature's spell to do what a woman must do.

He pushed again, felt a slight give; her lips tightened. He pushed, felt the widening. He was moving into her now. There was no two ways about it. He felt himself half-buried in her. He looked down. Her eyes were shut; she looked as if her whole being was concentrated on what was happening to her body. And her face was tight.

He moved, felt the gush, the wetness, and then went deep into her.

She groaned; it was pain but, more, a touch of pleasure. Now his hands held her buttocks and he began movement gently, in and out, over and over, pausing, kissing and caressing her body, his hands touching the magic places that nature had put there for the lady's pleasure. She seemed to be in a dream, just waiting.

Then his body, bursting with male force, thrust and thrust, and he felt the great swelling and a spurt of passion.

She felt it, and for the first time let out a smothered

gasp, a strange mixture of anguish and pleasure.

Then she flung her arms around him, pulled him to her body in a tight frenzy, stayed like that, as if she never wanted to let go.

The scream, Slocum felt, had told the men outside what had happened. As he came off her body, she let go reluctantly.

Then it hit him again: the mystery of why they'd given him this prize. They had to be crazy to give him Charity for destroying their brother.

Or did they have something devilish in mind? Something he couldn't even imagine?

The door opened and Red's bulky figure stood there, his gun in hand, a vicious leer on his face. He threw their clothing on the floor, picked up the chemise, and with a quick, brutal movement rubbed it in the small ripple of blood on Charity's thigh.

When Slocum moved, he pointed his gun, his eyes cruel. "Go ahead, gimme an excuse."

Then he backed off and growled. "Get your clothes on fast. We're travelling."

They had barely had time to dress when the men stomped in. Using short rope, Clem tied their wrists and pulled them out into the night. They lifted Charity onto a gelding and Slocum on his roan. Jessie held the reins of both horses as they started to ride northwest through the night.

Although the light was dim from a clouded moon, Red seemed to know the trail and they rode past silent twisted trees, rocks and slopes with deep shadows until the land went flat. They reached the outskirts of a big spread with buildings and corrals. It was late, and the ranch hands were asleep.

Slocum shook his head, baffled at the happenings of this night. What the hell was going on? What the hell was the point of all this?

They pulled up, tethered the horses to a tree, and Red drew his gun. "Not a word, not a whisper, or you're dead."

They walked quietly to within fifty yards of the big house in which a small light gleamed. Then Jessie made them sit and tied them back to back.

Red looked at them, his smile evil. "You're going to get a real sweet reward, Slocum, for doing what you did." He threw the blood-stained chemise on the ground nearby. For a long moment Red stared at Slocum, then his face distorted with rage. He swung his fist with all his force, but Slocum twisted his head, and the blow ripped his cheek and the blood gushed. Red grinned, then walked off jauntily, followed by the others.

Slocum heard them mount their horses, start to gallop, then the crack of their gunfire pierced the night. It did what they wanted—alerted the men in the ranch, and lights went on in some buildings.

Slocum's jaw hardened. If he got the chance, he'd pay the Dalton bunch back for their dirty work this night. He could hear muted voices coming from the big building, and he felt the girl's back stiffen against his.

"Damn it," he said, "are you going to tell me why they did this to you?"

After a long moment, she spoke in a low voice. "It's all because of Tad Dalton, the youngest brother."

Slocum waited; he had bad premonitions.

"Two weeks ago," she said, "I was riding out of town toward the ranch. This is the O'Rourke ranch, where I live. Tad Dalton had come out of the saloon drunk. He followed me, caught me on the trail, and tried to rape me. One of our ranch hands heard me yell and Tad Dalton ran off. My father and some men tracked Tad down." She stopped.

"What happened?"

Her voice was hoarse, shaky. "They castrated him."

The words hit Slocum with a shock. His eyes fastened on the bloody chemise lying a few feet away. He felt a sudden chill.

So that was the game Red was playing:

A sliver of moon peered through the dark night clouds.

Red's brother, Seth, had been shot by Slocum; and his younger brother, Tad, had been castrated by Charity's father.

Now with one trick Red had squared accounts. The sight of a violated daughter would put the rancher O'Rourke in a rage. And if O'Rourke would castrate a man who *tried* rape, what would he do to the man who, in his eyes, had succeeded?

Slocum felt another icy chill.

He could hear the soft sound of heavy boots, still far off. He didn't have a gun and he was tied like a hog for slaughter.

"Nice boys, that Dalton bunch," he said.

"Rotten to the core," Charity said.

"So, with one stroke they revenged their brothers."

"One stroke?"

"They paid you off for what happened to Tad Dalton. And hope to pay me off for what I did to Seth Dalton."

"Pay you off? What do you mean?"

He took a deep breath. "What do you suppose your

dad is going to do when he sees that bloody thing there?"

It was then he saw the big hulking forms come out of the shadows of the night.

Five men came stomping toward them, two out front, three twenty yards back. The two had their guns out and the big man in front, when he saw Slocum and the girl on the ground, cursed softly. He bent low and spoke in a gravelly voice. "Who is that? Is it Miss Charity, for God's sake?" He was broad-shouldered, big-chested, and he sounded amazed.

"Yes, Amos, it is."

He whistled softly, thought a moment, then turned to the other man, staring with his mouth open. "Frank, send the boys back. I don't want 'em to see this. And tell Mr. O'Rourke I asked for him to come out. Do it pronto."

"Is she all right, Amos?"

"Who the hell knows? Do as I say. Hurry, damn it."

Slocum watched Frank head off the other cowboys who peered in the dark, trying to make out the figures on the ground. Amos bent down and in a worried voice asked, "You all right, Miss Charity?" Probably the foreman, Slocum thought.

"All right, Amos," she said wearily.

Then Amos saw the bloody chemise, scowled, and walked over to pick it up. Slocum heard the deep growl in his throat. It's a bad setup, Slocum thought, and could get worse very fast. He watched Amos stuff the chemise inside his vest, walk slowly back for a closer look. His face was beefy, big-boned, his eyes big, staring.

"Who are you, mister?"

"Slocum, John Slocum. Will you cut these ropes, Amos?"

"Well, Slocum, maybe you better tell me what the hell all this means—you two tied together like this."

A stinking situation, Slocum thought. "A couple of polecats dropped us off, partner. Cut me loose. I aim to go after them."

Amos rubbed his chin. "I can't do a thing like that till Mr. O'Rourke gets here."

"Amos," said Charity, "cut these ropes."

There was a long pause. "I'm surely sorry, Miss Charity, but I think your father should see all this before I do a thing. He'd tan my hide otherwise."

It's getting worse, thought Slocum, as he saw a bulky man wearing a stetson and his jeans over his longjohns come hurrying toward them. He stopped ten feet away and stared at what had to be an amazing spectacle, his daughter and a husky stranger tied together on the ground. He was speechless for a moment, then turned. "Why the hell don't you cut them apart, Amos?" His voice was harsh and deep.

"I wanted you to see it, Mr. O'Rourke."

"Who the hell wants to see *that?*"

Then Amos pulled the chemise from under his vest, moved to huddle with O'Rourke, spoke in low tones. O'Rourke stared at the chemise, thunderstruck. Then he looked at Slocum, and shook, as if in a spasm of fury. If he had a gun, Slocum felt, he'd have blasted him right there.

"Cut them ropes." His voice was harsh, his fists clenched.

Amos pulled a knife from its holster and slashed the ropes. Slocum stood up, moving his arms, stomping his legs, which felt almost numb.

In the glimmering light of the moon, O'Rourke's face was one great scowl. It was a broad-boned, beefy face with glowing brown eyes. "What in the blazes happened to you, Charity?"

The girl gazed at her father, her face twisted with grief, then rushed to him. "Oh, Dad!"

Slocum's teeth clenched; that gesture spoke volumes. O'Rourke would see it as a daughter hurt, shamed, maybe degraded.

O'Rourke turned to Amos. "Gimme your gun." His mind, Slocum could tell, was no longer on his daughter. He took the Colt from Amos, pointed it at Slocum, then spoke slowly.

"Start talking, mister."

Slocum cleared his throat. What the hell could he say? That bloody chemise said it all. "It's hard to tell it. Red Dalton put a gun on me. He forced the play."

O'Rourke leaned forward. "Who?" his voice was strangled hoarse.

"Red Dalton."

There was a thunderous moment of silence, and Slocum could see the artery in O'Rourkes's neck begin to pump. He spoke slowly. "So Red Dalton put a gun on you. And you raped my little girl. Well, you shoulda let him shoot you, because there are some things worse than dying."

Slocum stood quiet. O'Rourke was a bull of a man, jealous of his daughter's honor. He had castrated Tad Dalton. And he might hate Red Dalton for what he'd just done, but he could never tolerate the idea that a stranger had violated his little girl. It didn't matter a damn that Slocum had been forced. All he would see was that some wandering polecat had fouled the purity of his beloved Charity. Slocum should have died first.

Charity, who'd been listening as if she didn't understand her father, spoke.

"For God's sake, Dad, it wasn't his fault. He tried to avoid it."

O'Rourke turned, glared at her, then snarled, "Did I ask your opinion?"

"You don't understand, Dad. He was forced. Dalton had a gun on him. Woulda killed him." A gutsy filly, Slocum thought, just as he'd expected.

"Then he shoulda let himself be killed," O'Rourke roared, the veins in his neck engorged. He turned to Amos and Frank. "Lock him up till morning. Then we'll turn this stallion into a canary."

Charity stared at him in horror. "For God's sake, Dad, don't you understand? He was *forced*. I wasn't going to let him die because of me."

He swung around and slapped her face in rage. "Shut up! I don't want another word outa you. You're a piece of damaged goods now." He pushed her in front of him, scowling. "As for that Dalton bunch, it's goin' to be a sorry day for them, come tomorrow."

A brawny, thick-nosed cowboy they called Dogface Jim brought him under his gun to something like a storehouse, near the stable. He was pushed roughly into it.

"We'll take care of your nuggets in the morning, Slocum," Dogface said with a horrible grin as he shut the door and turned the key.

It was dark and Slocum couldn't make out the walls. A musty smell of hay hit his nostrils and it put him in mind of the barn back in Calhoun County when as a boy, sweaty and tired, he lay in the hay and dreamed about the future. But this was not a time to get into the past. He scouted the room; no windows, solid, thick walls. He'd be tight in this lockup till morning, and that meant a nasty visit from O'Rourke and his men.

"We'll turn this stallion into a canary," O'Rourke had said, and even the thought chilled Slocum's blood. Women had meant lots of good times, and to be deprived of the means of enjoying them must be the worst thing in the world. His nerves tightened and he roamed the room like a caged lion. Again and again he tested the wood, looking for a soft spot to cut through with the thin-bladed knife concealed in his boot. But the wood was solid oak. Twice he tried talking to Dogface, but that dumb ox had been swilling booze and now he snored with the sounds of a slaughtered bull. Sweat crawled under Slocum's collar as time pushed on. Again he shuffled in the dark from one end of the room to the other. He felt like a rat in a trap, felt the walls closing in on him. It was hot, the air rotten, his body sweated. No point wasting energy; he'd sit on the floor and wait. He couldn't break out and that was a fact. He sat in the dark, too tense to sleep, and then he heard something.

It couldn't be morning; he wasn't ready for that. The sound when it came again was someone on tiptoe. He held his breath.

The snoring stopped, then came a bunch of guttural curses.

"Why'd you take my gun, Miss Charity?"

"Open the door, Jim."

"I can't do that, Miss Charity."

"Open it, Jim."

"Your father would skin me, Miss Charity."

"Just tell him I aimed to put a bullet in your leg, and you don't care to be a cripple because of nothing at all. That man in there is no criminal. Now open the door. I'll give you one minute, then I'll shoot."

There was grumbling, then a rattle, and the door swung open. Slocum reached out, pulled Dogface Jim into the room, and hit his jaw. His knees buckled, and he dropped like a log of wood. Slocum took the key from him, shut the door. Dogface's gun was on the ground. Slocum scooped it up and felt a surge of power. He took a deep breath; locked in and without the gun, he'd been like a lion without teeth. He leaned forward, pulled Charity to him, and hugged her. "One of the nicest things you ever did, honey."

Her lovely mouth twisted in a smile. "I couldn't let them do a hurt like *that* to you, Slocum, 'specially because of me."

He grinned. "It'd be a crime against nature. Now, my horse. Would it be nearby?"

She led the way. It was still dark, but strains of grey were streaking the sky. The roan nuzzled his shoulder and Slocum ran his hand affectionately over the muscular haunches. His companion, his loyal friend. He swung the saddle over its back.

Charity had come up alongside. "I'm going, too, you know." Her voice was firm.

He stared. "No, you just stay put."

"I won't be able to after this. My father..."

"Oh, yes, you will. You're the apple of his eye."

Her lips tightened. "He treats me like a girl. I can't take it." She smiled. "I'm a woman now. You did it."

He gritted his teeth. "Listen, I'm going after the Dalton bunch. With you hanging on, it'd be impossible."

She threw her head back. "I ride as good as any man. I've got a gelding that will outrun anything. And I've got a grievance against Red Dalton, too."

He shook his head. She had a lot of spirit, but she wasn't thinking too good. He straightened up in the saddle. "You're a beautiful young lady, Charity, but you belong at home. This is no trip for you. I don't want you hurt. So goodbye."

He moved the roan out quietly and turned south.

2

The Daltons' prints raced toward Red Creek, a small town which, from Slocum's view on the high slope, looked like it was planted on a flat plain as it broiled in the sun. Slocum too felt the heat and he loosened his red kerchief to mop the sweat from his face.

He thought of the Daltons, Red and Clem, and their cousin Jessie, three gunslingers with mangy ideas. They had grabbed an innocent young girl, forced her into sex, then tried to put his own balls under the hammer. For all that they deserved a reward, and he had it in his holster.

He stared at Red Creek, a cluster of rough-cut houses with a saloon in the center of main street. The Daltons would stop there for a quick pickup, but they'd move on. They were after something.

He nudged the roan. Did the Daltons know he was

trailing them? His smile was hard. No, by this time they figured he'd be minus his family jewels. They figured that O'Rourke, a raging bull, would grab instant revenge. They had to figure, too, that O'Rourke and his men would come after them hot and heavy.

The dust on the street stirred gently as Slocum walked the roan to Reardon's saloon. He flipped the reins at the post and pushed in the batwing doors. A spacious saloon with men playing cards at two tables, two women sitting at a table with a brawny, curly-haired cowboy, and three booted men standing at the bar. No sign of the Daltons.

Everyone threw a glance at him, the new face in town. The barkeep, Reardon, came over, a beet-faced man with black slicked-down hair.

"Whiskey," said Slocum.

Reardon put a bottle and a glass in front of Slocum, leaned his elbow on the bar, and smiled, showing yellow crooked teeth. "Hot day, mister."

"The name is Slocum." He filled the glass, threw his head back as he gulped the whiskey. It burned the dust off his throat. "Hell is always hot," he said.

Reardon grinned. "That's Texas, Slocum. Where yuh headed?"

"It depends."

A lean, lantern-jawed cowboy at the bar spoke up. "If you're going west, Slocum, keep an eye peeled. The Comanches are ridin'. They ripped up the Baker homestead. The Bakers weren't there, but they got horses and whiskey."

Slocum nodded, then leaned toward Reardon. "See anything of the Dalton bunch?"

Reardon's eyes glittered. "Yeah, we seen them."

Slocum waited. Then Reardon said, "They drank

a lotta booze, then started shootin' up the glasses to show how good they were."

That would be the Daltons, Slocum thought. "Say where they were heading?"

Reardon stroked his chin. "Maybe Jessie told Dolly Marsh. He went upstairs to tell Dolly Marsh how much he thought of her." He smiled. "Dolly's the redhead."

Slocum turned to look at the women. They wore red dresses with ruffles and low-cut fronts that flashed a lot of silky white skin and breast. He looked at Dolly, sitting next to the curly-headed cowboy. Her face was like a doll's, with round blue eyes and a cupid's mouth that smiled at him.

Slocum fingered his glass. She looked like a nice roll in the hay; he might combine business with pleasure. Behind her the stairs went up to the rooms in which the ladies entertained their customers. He poured another shot, considering.

Dolly, with the instinct of a woman who knew when she'd snared a customer, watched him. He smiled, and she smiled back, showing brilliant teeth. He pointed upstairs and she nodded, holding her smile. The cowboy sitting with the women scowled, his blue eyes stony on Slocum. He gritted his teeth when Dolly, without a word, stood and started for the stairs. Curly wore a Colt and beat-up chaps, and when Slocum, bottle in hand, walked past, he glared belligerently.

"Where in hell you headin', mister?" he growled.

Everyone turned to look. The players at the table paused in their play.

Slocum stopped. "You're not polite, sonny," he said pleasantly. "But since you're interested, I'm going up to pay my respects to the young lady."

The cowboy's eyes narrowed. "You ain't going upstairs. You're going out the door and on your way, mister."

Slocum had to smile. "And why do you think that?"

Curly grimaced. "'Cause I don't like anyone criticizing my manners. Don't like you much either."

Slocum shook his head. He had nothing against this cowboy, too big for his britches, who was showing uncalled-for jealousy about a saloon party girl.

"Well," he drawled, "if you want to be a bad-mannered brat, it's okay with me. But I aim to go up those stairs."

Curly flushed and stood up slowly. "I just told you to get on your horse and keep going."

Slocum sighed. There was always a rambunctious young cowboy eager to prove himself a stallion. Somehow, he kept running into such men. Slocum was sturdy and big, and many a tenderfoot figured if he knocked Slocum down he'd establish his manhood.

The bar was silent, ready for an interesting play.

Slocum studied the cocky cowboy. He was young, foolish, maybe had too many hard whiskies. Slocum didn't care for the idea of a shootout.

"Are you going to pull your gun on a small thing like this?" he asked.

Curly shook his head. "Naw, mister, I'm just going to nail your ears back." He started to roll up his sleeves, showing a hefty bicep.

"Could I ask you to back off? This ain't necessary," Slocum said grimly.

"I don't back off," Curly sneered, as if he suspected Slocum was softening.

Slocum put the bottle on the table and turned to face Curly. He had a broad face with narrow blue eyes and a sullen, spoiled-brat face. Looked like he might be a dangerous brawler, but from his stance, Slocum didn't believe he had it yet. Slocum didn't care for a drag-down fight, so he closed his fists tight, feinted low with his left to bring down Curly's guard, then swung hard, putting his shoulder into it. Curly was jolted and his knees buckled. He looked amazed, then, shaking his head as if to clear it, he came forward, swinging wild. Slocum blocked his punches, feinted again, and swung an overpowering right at the point of the jaw. On target: Curly's eyes rolled into his head, and he went down like an empty sack.

Slocum shook his head regretfully, picked up the bottle, stepped past the fallen warrior, and climbed the stairs toward Dolly who had been watching from the balcony with shining eyes.

She said nothing and he followed her to the third door.

The room had a big bed, a small table, two glasses, a pitcher, and a square mirror on the wall. The window faced the main street, and from it Slocum could see a great stretch of land patched with brush, trees, and rocks.

Dolly poured the whiskey into two glasses. Her skin looked silky and her lush red hair fell to her shoulders. She had blue eyes with green specks, and now her Cupid's-bow mouth smiled.

"You're good with your hands, Slocum."

"I may be good with something else, if you're a nice girl."

"Wouldn't surprise me." She sipped the whiskey. "Can't understand why Curly acted so stupid. But he can be ornery."

"It's jealousy," said Slocum. "He wants you all to himself."

"Yeah, but he can't afford it." Her face was grim.

"I'm looking for the Dalton bunch," Slocum said. "I hear tell that Jessie came through here. Do you know him?"

Her smile froze. "Yeah, I know him." She lifted her whiskey glass, but her eyes stayed on him. "Is that what you're here for?"

"It's part of what I'm here for." He waited.

"Jessie Dalton is a rough customer," she said finaly.

"How rough?"

She gulped her whiskey, put the cup on the table, then deliberately unbuttoned her blouse. Her heavy breasts swung out, but she turned to show her back. There were red bruises.

"That rough." She closed her dress, poured another whiskey. "He was drunk, but the real man came through."

Slocum scowled. "Why'd he do that?"

Her lip curled. "Had trouble getting started, like it was my fault. Or maybe it's the *way* he gets started."

Slocum's jaw hardened. "A pig of a man. Did he say where he was headed?"

"No, he didn't say that."

"What did he say?"

"He said I reminded him of a bitch named Maude, that she, too, had red hair, that she was a greedy little slut, and that he was going to nail her to a tree."

Slocum nodded. "Nice fella, this Jessie."

"They're hyenas, the Daltons. You aiming to tackle them—just you?"

"Just me."

She studied him, and her blue eyes gleamed. "You got guts, but I'm not sure you're smart. They're gunslingers, each one, and ornery clear through."

He watched her pouring a drink for him, her blue eyes shining, her mouth in a tight smile. She glanced at the bed. "I was saying you can really use your hands."

"Yeah, I can use them." He moved to her, loosened her dress, and suddenly her breasts were out. They were hefty, silky-looking, with pouting nipples. He fondled them for a while, then pulled her toward the bed, sat on it, and put his tongue to the nipple. She sighed, watched him for a while, then slipped to the floor. "What you got hiding there?" she asked coyly, and her eyes went round as she looked at his swollen potency. She put her palm around it, stroked it, gazed at him, her eyes smoldering. "The answer to a woman's dream," she murmured, and, leaning forward, put her lips to it. She did some fancy work, then Slocum, feeling the mounting tension, withdrew, and they pulled off the rest of their clothes. She was built solidly, a sensual body with rounded hips, well-shaped legs, her red hair scarcely hiding the pink crease. Her buttocks were so beautifully shaped that he put her on the bed with her plump cheeks facing him. He slipped between the silky full cheeks to the moist crease between them and held her hips. He moved, and she gasped as the full size of him slipped completely into her.

He held her breasts, then began his movements, a rhythm that she picked up, and, as they went on and on, the pleasure of it kept climbing, and she would scream a bit to herself, while he felt the surging inside her. Then, as his tension soared, he thrust harder, feeling a great swelling as he hit the peak. She screeched through her clenched teeth.

Then she lay under him, her plump buttocks pressed

against his belly, and he felt his excitement slowly subside.

The step on the stairs was soft, but he heard it and his hand moved even before his brain registered the danger, and he had the Colt, always near him, and was waiting when the door was suddenly kicked open. There was Curly, gun in hand, ready to shoot, but Slocum's bullet hit his wrist and the gun fell from his hand. He grabbed at his wrist, stared at Dolly's nude body, then, his eyes glaring with hate, he bent slowly to retrieve the gun with his left hand. Slocum watched him start to bring the gun up for another shot, and fired again, and Curly hurtled back, a bullet in his left shoulder; he lay in the hall, quiet, mostly in shock, not fatally wounded.

Slocum cursed and climbed into his jeans, pulling them over his body still in the sweat of his encounter with Dolly. "Won't let a man screw in peace these days," he growled as he bent to look at Curly. Then he mumbled, "A born fool."

The sun was a blaze of orange in a steel-bright sky as Slocum rode toward Sweetwater. From the hurried tracks, he could tell the Daltons were sweating their horses. Surely they couldn't be running from him; they had to believe that O'Rourke, being a jealous bull about his daughter, had by this time turned Slocum into a soprano. No, the Daltons were running either from O'Rourke's revenge or toward something real hot.

His mind, as he rode, slipped back to Charity and he had to smile. She was one gutsy filly, the way she stood up to her fire-snorting father and the way she pulled a gun on Dogface. O'Rourke would probably blister her butt for that. "You're a piece of damaged goods," he had yelled at her. A nice daddy.

Slocum shifted uncomfortably in the saddle. She'd stuck her neck out for him, and it was a pity to leave her at the mercy of O'Rourke. But she'd bog him down, he'd have to worry about her, and with gunslingers like the Daltons, you didn't lose your concentration, not for a moment.

Slocum tried never to lose his concentration. It had made him a survivor in the War, and up to now had kept him alive in a raw territory that pulled, like a magnet, the bad men of the country. In this territory a man had to have the instinct to smell a threat and a fast gun to kill it—or else . . .

As he rode, his eyes moved restlessly, probing for Comanche ambush. He'd seen the lone print of an unshod pony, a day old, two miles back at the water creek. Some wandering brave, perhaps. But mostly, he stayed aware of the Dalton prints. Suddenly he frowned and pulled the roan to a halt. The Daltons had stopped here to palaver, the prints showed it, and a smoked cheroot on the earth. Then they split, two horses to the west, one to the north. Why? To the north, he knew of a stagecoach depot at Twin Fork. Well, he'd follow the single rider. Real thoughtful of them to give him one target: easier than facing three. The two riders west must be headed for Sweetwater. All the prints were fresh.

He put the roan into a hard run and, at Twin-Fork it took only minutes to learn Jessie Dalton had gone hard-riding after the stagecoach.

He picked up the trail, his mind working on this puzzle. The stagecoach was headed for Sweetwater, and the two Daltons riding west were on a trail to

crisscross it. There was a scheme to nail that stagecoach, one from behind, two from the north. Why?
The Daltons were gunslingers, but this coach carried
no money, just passengers. Were they also petty
thieves? It hardly seemed likely. But it might be a
good time to hit them while they tangled with the
stagecoach.

He raced toward the butte which bulked heavily
to the west. He knew an old Indian trail, a passage
through the rocks, a shortcut to pick up the trail used
by the stagecoach to reach Sweetwater.

When he reached the climb, he gave the roan its
head, letting it pick its own way over the tricky, rocky
trail. The sun threw its pitiless rays on the boulders
on either side of him. The back muscles of the roan
gleamed with sweat, and his own shirt felt drenched.
After a half hour of this tricky riding he swung off
the saddle, poured water from his canteen into his hat,
and let the roan drink. The big brown eyes of the
horse looked at him and Slocum felt a rush of affection. "Old pal," he muttered, and patted the powerful
neck. Then Slocum loosened his neckerchief, mopped
the sweat from his face. He took a mouthful of water
from the canteen, mounted up, and started the climb
again.

The sun was a blistering eye in a scorched sky
when he reached the top of the trail, sandwiched between giant crags. He slipped off the saddle, took his
Winchester, and crawled forward to peer down at the
landscape. A plain with boulders stretched for a mile,
and beyond it, a stand of cottonwoods. The trail ran
alongside the butte, and the stagecoach pulled frantically by four horses came thundering along. The
driver, a man wearing a black sombrero, was cracking

his whip and glancing fearfully behind at a rider on a sorrel waving a gun. Slocum recognized Jessie Dalton and instantly he started to move down the rocky trail to get closer. Then he saw the other Daltons, Red and Clem, on their big blacks, racing from the north, aiming to block the stagecoach. A crisscross, Slocum thought, just as he had figured. The Daltons wanted to nail that wagon.

The driver had sighted the trap and began to flay his horses. They were big-chested and great runners, and under the whip they snorted and galloped and, to Slocum's surprise, began to pull away from the Daltons.

Slocum, because he felt himself too far for a clean shot, kept coming down, moving light, staying behind the boulders. He could see one passenger in a wide-brimmed hat and frock coat lean out the jostling wagon, trying to potshoot Jessie Dalton. By now the coach had reached directly below Slocum's position on the butte. Suddenly Red Dalton pulled up on his big horse and grabbed his rifle. There was the echo of gunfire off the rocks and then the driver of the coach jerked crazily, stood up, and somersaulted off the careening wagon. He hit the earth dead as a log.

No longer goaded by the whip, the horses slowed up, and the Daltons fired to keep the passengers hunkered down until Jessie caught up with the coach, scrambled from the back to the driver's seat, and pulled the team to a snorting halt.

Slocum's face was grim as he worked to get into range where he might do some damage. These Daltons were mangy dogs, and there had to be a vicious payoff for them to sweat like this to nail the stagecoach.

The Daltons surrounded the coach, guns pointing,

and yelled at the passengers to come out with their hands up. The man in the wide-brimmed hat, a woman in a blue shirt, and two brawny cowhands in jeans and boots emerged.

Red studied them, a demonic grin on his face. "Throw your guns," he yelled, and Slocum, crouched by a boulder, was astonished how clearly the sound, lifted by wind, reached his ears.

The cowboys threw their guns and scowled, expecting a holdup. The man in the frock coat moved slowly, as if the last thing he wanted was to drop his Colt. But Red, grinning diabolically, put his gun at the man's chest, and the man dropped his gun.

Red looked at Clem, and Clem gazed thoughtfully at the two cowhands. Then, without lifting an eyebrow, he fired four times and the two cowhands hurtled back as if kicked by a mule, and fell on their backs as crimson rushed to stain their shirts.

Slocum cursed softly, shocked at such cold-blooded killings. He gritted his teeth and moved down quietly and as fast as he could.

Then Red turned to the man in the frock coat and grinned. "Well, Devlan, this is your lucky day. We finally caught up with you and your bitch."

The three Daltons then crowded Devlan, but because of a shift of wind and their lowered voices, Slocum could no longer hear.

Red seemed to want something from Devlan, but he wanted to bargain. Red spoke to the woman and, angered by her reply, slapped her. Devlan, infuriated, started for Red, but Jessie put a gun to his head. Red bared his teeth, obviously in a rage, and seemed to be delivering an ultimatum. Devlan squeezed out some words, and Red, again angered, swung at his jaw, knocking him down. The woman went for Red, clawing at him and forcing him back. Clem brutally pulled her off and punched her, which left her stunned. Then Clem ripped at her shirt and bared her breasts. Red and Jessie, guns pointing, grinning, watched Devlan as Clem overpowered the woman and stripped her naked. And Slocum, as he moved into range, couldn't help admiring her body, its well-formed breasts, slender waist, rounded hips, the dark hair between her thighs.

Clem, brutish and heavy-shouldered, grinned viciously as he opened his jeans. He liked to be rough with women. And what he was doing was not only an act of violence against her, but against Devlan, whose features were distorted in hopeless rage.

Slocum watched Clem force the woman down, his movements brutal. Slocum, seething with anger, sighted his rifle and squeezed the trigger. The crack bounced against the rocks as the bullet crashed through Clem's head, spewing his brains on the earth. His body shuddered in a spasm and went still.

The other Daltons dropped to the ground. Red, with quick reflex, flashed a shot at the rocks, though he couldn't possibly see the target, a strategic shot that made Slocum by instinct duck for cover. It gave the Daltons time to scramble behind the coach. They had no way of knowing how many men were on the cliffside. A gunshot and a cry pierced the air and Slocum peered from behind a boulder. Devlan was down. Two shots splintered the stone near him; they had him spotted.

He crouched and tried to figure his next move. They had two guns, but he had superior position. Finally, he crawled flat behind another boulder and peered out and, to his astonishment, saw the two Daltons on their horses swinging behind the scattered boulders, which protected them from gunfire. Why he wondered, hadn't they stayed to shoot it out? Well, maybe they had what they wanted: Devlan dead. The woman, bent down, was looking at him. And by now the Daltons were out of gun range, running their horses west, toward Sweetwater. No hurry; he'd pick them up there.

He started down the jagged side of the cliff and the going was slow. The woman was grim-faced as she examined Devlan. She saw Slocum coming, then, aware of her nakedness, she went to her clothes and moved behind a nearby rock. By the time he reached the bottom of the cliff she had her clothing on and was back with the dead man, her face distorted with strain.

"The bastards," she said between clenched teeth. "The rotten bastards."

Slocum looked around. Four men were sprawled in death near the stagecoach; Clem, two cowboys in buckskins, Devlan. Back further lay the driver of the stagecoach.

It meant a big grave.

3

It had been two hours since he had dropped the dead men in the mass grave, and they had been riding on the Dalton tracks toward Sweetwater. She was on Clem Dalton's horse, a big-chested sorrel, and until he reached this small stream where he stopped to let the horses drink, she'd been moody and silent. Now she spoke. "I'm Maude McKay, and thanks for what you did."

He nodded. "The name's John Slocum, and it was a pleasure to do it, Miss Maude." The sun was sliding down in the sky, and he thought they might stop for a bit. He made a fire, heated some coffee. After sipping it, she seemed relaxed.

For the first time he could look closely at her: a damned good-looking woman with glowing dark eyes, a high-boned, smooth face, a wide-lipped mouth, and a fully packed body under her shirt and tight riding jeans. He'd seen the body and had to admit it was damned sexy.

She gazed at him over her cup of coffee. "Could I ask you how you happened to be in the right spot at the right time?"

"Trying to catch up with the Daltons," he said. "And you happened to be in trouble when I caught up."

A small smile. "Mighty lucky for me." Her face tightened. "Pity you didn't get them before they got Devlan." Her gaze was curious. "Could I ask why you're after the Daltons?"

He pulled out a havana, scratched a lucifier with his thumbnail, and lit it. Not an easy thing to tell a woman, he thought, but she looked like a woman who'd knocked about a bit and knew the evil in men.

"To tell it quick, they were trying to get me castrated."

Her eyes opened with shock, then quickly slipped down to the bunchup in his jeans. "That's a hell of a thing to do to a man," she said finally. "'Course, there are men who deserve it." She looked at him intently. "And it's the last thing a woman would want to happen to *some* men."

"I'll take that as a compliment," he grinned.

"And you should. But tell me, Mr. Slocum, why'd they want to do you such a cruel mischief?"

He rubbed his chin and looked up. The sun, a huge red ball, hung at the bottom of the flame-colored sky. A lone eagle flew west, swinging its powerful wings slowly, probably headed to its nest among the peaks of the bulking mountain.

"It's too long a story to tell now. I'd like to get

closer to Sweetwater before we lose daylight. There are still two Daltons fouling up the country."

He brought over Clem's big sorrel, which had been grazing nearby, and held it while Maude swung over the horse. She sat nicely, and he couldn't help but note how neatly her rump fitted on the saddle. He clamped his teeth; he'd seen her buxom body, and the image stuck in his head and somehow kept perturbing his loins.

He swung over the big roan and followed the Dalton trail which went northwest. They rode through a lush meadow carpeted with yellow daffodils, and a light, fragrant breeze played over his face, welcome relief from the blistering heat of the day. As the sun went lower, and the peaks and crags caught a sudden glint of gold, he watched it with pleasure. *This is God's country,* he thought, *big and beautiful.* Only men soiled it, men like the Daltons. They'd just killed two passengers in that stagecoach, witnesses shot down in cold blood who happened to be in the wrong place. They wanted to make Devlan talk and started to rape Maude. Men like the Daltons were the scum of the earth, and if he did nothing else, he'd dedicate himself to their destruction.

He thought of Maude and hoped she'd volunteer what the Daltons wanted from Devlan, but she didn't. Soon it would be too dark to follow the Dalton tracks. The sun had gone down, and dark clouds were stealing across the sky. He moved to a small stream near where they could pitch camp and let the horses drink. Then he tensed. The prints of two unshod ponies were at the water edge. Comanche!

He swung off the saddle. The prints looked about a day old, and came out the other side of the stream, going east. Two braves on a hunt? Or were they just prowling in paleface territory to spread mayhem? He should make sure.

"Wait here," he said.

She frowned. "Where are you going?"

"I want to see what's over there. Want to sleep and not wake up to find my throat cut. Just rest easy." He followed the prints and they moved to hilly timber ground. Then he saw the blood smear and tracks of a wild pig. Hunting, he decided. But where did they camp? The prints went up higher, to the rocks. On their way east. He couldn't follow them: he was after the Daltons. He nudged the roan and came back to where Maude sat easy against a cottonwood. It was a good sheltered area, a good place to bed down for the night. He pulled the beef jerky, opened a can of peaches, dug a pit to hide the fire, and made coffee.

The dark came fast, a quarter-moon that started to climb, and the sky glittered soon with a million stars. The moonlight shone on the smooth skin of her face and her eyes looked deep and dark.

He sipped his coffee. "What the hell was happening back there, Maude? The Daltons sure had a big grievance against your friend Devlan."

She looked away. "The Daltons didn't need a grievance. They're just naturally ornery."

He frowned. "Yeah, they're ornery, but they were putting a hard squeeze on Devlan. Why was that?"

She just sat silent. After a time she looked at him, and something in his face pushed her. "What difference does it make, Slocum? You aim to get the Daltons anyway."

He grimaced. He'd saved her ass from a nasty wrestling match with Clem Dalton, but it seemed to have slipped her mind. The shriek of a night hawk pierced the quiet, then came the wail of a coyote, Boulders and trees cast dark mysterious shadows. Slocum was aware of it all; part of his mind checked the sounds and shadows for the one note that would mean danger, and part of his mind speculated on why she wouldn't talk.

"Yeah, I aim to get the Daltons," he said finally, "and they aim to get me. I reckon it won't hurt for me to know what they're after. When you hunt a bear, it helps to know the bear likes honey."

Her eyes were widely innocent. "You're spinning a big yarn about nothing."

"The Daltons went to a lot of trouble to get to you and your friend Devlan. They tracked and trapped that stagecoach. They shot the driver and two witnesses. They were about to rape you. It's mighty hard to believe it was because Devlan beat them in a game of dominoes."

She laughed. "You got a sense of humor, Slocum." She looked thoughtfully up at the moon, then back at him. "I'll tell you, all right. It's like this. Devlan sold the Daltons fifty head of cattle. It turned out later the cattle had the pox. Devlan didn't know it at the time, but the Daltons didn't believe him. Anyway, they wanted their money."

He stared. "Why didn't you tell this before? Why the mystery?"

Her dark eyes gazed calmly at him. "Devlan was someone I cared about. He'd just been shot. I wasn't in the mood to talk about it."

Slocum nodded slowly. It did make sense, and he felt a bit discomfited about pressing her. But later, when he lay on his bedroll and his eyes scanned the star-studded sky, the story left him unsatisfied. She was holding something back, he felt, and he didn't like it. The Daltons were tricky and dangerous; they were two and he was one. He'd caught them off guard this time, concentrating on the stagecoach: it had given him an edge. But now they knew he was on their tail and they'd be ready. He needed whatever help he could get, and Maude McKay was not giving him any.

Then, from the other side of the cottonwood, where she'd put her bedroll, he heard her voice. "I'd like to thank you again, Slocum. Clem Dalton was one loco wolf. I'd hate to think what would have happened without your gun."

He lifted himself on his elbow. She seemed to want to patch things up; maybe she had a guilty conscience.

"That story about the cattle and the pox," he said. "Were you straight on that?"

A moment of silence. "Why should you think otherwise, Slocum?" She turned her back and pulled the blanket over her.

His jaw tightened. "Why won't you tell the true reason the Daltons came gunning for you both?"

Not a sound. He leaned back on his bedroll, put his hands behind his head. "Perhaps you'll talk before we get to Sweetwater," he said softly.

Just before daybreak Slocum came alert. He had heard the soft step of Maude toward her horse. Though his eyes stayed shut, his ears followed her moves. She was going to make a break. Why? Didn't want to stick around because he pressed her too hard?

He should stop her; it was dangerous country. But it might be smart to let her go. Maybe her moves would explain the riddle of Devlan. He listened to the sound of a horse on soft earth, led quietly west. Sweetwater. Yes, he'd let her go, get more sleep, pick her up later. He slept for a while until the dull grey of daylight pushed out the dark.

By the time the sun had flooded the sky with the red of dawn, he was not far behind her. She had stayed on the Daltons' tracks.

He rode, as usual, always scanning the earth, and his skin suddenly prickled. The prints of an unshod pony, from out of a cluster of cottonwoods, cutting Maude's trail.

He studied the prints and his green eyes slitted. The prints were fresh, meaning the Comanche had either seen her or judged from the light prints of the sorrel that the rider was a woman.

Slocum cursed silently. He should have stopped her. He had known last night about two Comanches. Where was the other? They had been hunting. Had he gone back to the tribe with the game? He would be here otherwise, wouldn't he? Even one Comanche could be a vicious challenge. He put the roan into a run. Something bad could happen in a hurry unless Maude was lucky. She'd escaped from Clem Dalton, and though the Daltons were rotten coyotes, there wouldn't have been a killing. Even they didn't go that far with women. But a Comanche filled with hate for the palefaces who killed his buffalo, his brothers, wiped out his women and children in their camps— the Comanche would be an avenging devil. He would not only rape her but scalp her, brutally tomahawk her. Slocum had seen such things. It would be revenge for the Comanche, for the wrongs done to his way of life. A single Comanche prowling about could have one aim: to do as much damage as he could.

He pushed the roan harder, his eyes searching the land restlessly.

When he reached a steep slope, he charged up hard for a wide view, and at the top he jumped off the roan and crawled ahead. Then he saw Maude on her sorrel, riding nice and leisurely on the trail next to a sharp rise of rocks and trees. He shook his head in wonder. She led a charmed life, riding like that, blithely unaware that for some time she'd been the target of a bloodthirsty Comanche. For obscure reasons, the Indian had swung off her trail, maybe in pursuit of other prey.

And then, because Slocum was a careful man, his piercing green eyes slowly raked the surrounding terrain. He stiffened. Then he focused on a form, immovable as a rock, standing against a tree in perfect camouflage. He watched, scarcely breathing, studying the Comanche. Why was he frozen like that? To strike suddenly at her, like a coiled snake at a bird? Or was he waiting for Slocum because he had discovered a tracker and was about to spring a trap? Was it Maude or himself?

Slocum dared not move. If the Comanche aimed at the paleface squaw, he'd be little aware of much else. Even from this distance he looked powerful, his body muscular, with a red band tightly holding his long hair. Then, as if the temptation of a white squaw, lovely and alone, was too much for him, the Comanche started down the slope, flailing his spotted pony. He had a tomahawk in his hand and a knife in his belt.

Slocum swiftly brought the roan down the slope to the plain, put the spur to him, and the horse was quick to understand this would be an all-out run.

The Comanche came pounding hard, and Maude, hearing the hoofbeats, turned, her face in shock. She stared, then began to whip the sorrel frantically. The Comanche had come down only fifteen yards behind her, kicking his pony to a high burst of speed. He gained on the sorrel, and Slocum figured the Comanche would nail Maude in the next few minutes. He'd never get close enough to do any good, he thought, and reached behind to pull his Winchester from its holster. He watched the Comanche bring his pony alongside the sorrel and grab its reins. Maude swung at him. He ignored her, pulled hard on the reins, forcing the sorrel to a trembling halt. Maude kicked at the Comanche and he grabbed her leg, pulled it, and she came off the horse. Her impact against the earth stunned her, and the Comanche, big-chested, bronze-bodied, with fierce, blunt features, flung himself astride her, slapped her face hard twice, pulled her to her feet, tore off her shirt, and pulled at the rest of her clothes. She fought, trying to break away. He pulled his knife, waved it threateningly. She lay silent, fearful of death. The Comanche watched her closely, grinned fiendishly, then put the knife down, pushed her legs apart. He pulled down his breechclout, and leaned into her.

By this time Slocum had reached a point where he might shoot. The Comanche's struggle with Maude so preoccupied him that he could hardly be aware of anything else.

Slocum waited, holding his breath for the right moment. They were too close; he didn't have a shot.

Just then the Comanche, with a sixth sense, became aware of sounds he'd heard unconsciously and wheeled about and looked directly at Slocum. The bark of the rifle and at the same time a blob of red appeared on the Comanche's forehead. His body was hurtled away from Maude and he lay sprawled with his face against the earth.

Maude, naked, lay silent as if in shock, her eyes wide with fear. The sight of the suddenly dead Comanche seemed to have restored her senses. Slowly she sat up and looked at Slocum coming toward her. She shut her eyes, as if her feelings were too much. Then she stood up, her body white in the sun. He could see her shapely breasts, her wide hips, her slender waist. He realized this was the second time he'd seen her nude, that he'd shot a rapist off her body. He pulled a havana out of his chest pocket and lit it, smiling grimly. It was getting to be a habit; he seemed always to be in the neighborhood when someone was grabbing for Maude.

By the time he reached her, she'd slipped into her clothes, and though she still seemed shaky, she managed a smile.

"God, that was scary." She took a deep breath. "Mr. Slocum, this is the second time you have saved me. I realize now that I wasn't very smart to leave your protection this morning. If you forgive me, I promise not to leave your side until we get to Sweetwater."

4

He buried the Comanche and took pains to remove the tracks and signs of the grave. The last thing he wanted was for a wandering brave to discover a dead comrade and start a trail of vengeance. He smoothed the ground with a branch and pulled the pony behind them for half a mile, then turned it loose with a whack, hoping it would go wild and join a herd.

Maude, jolted by her close call with the Comanche, rode along quietly. Slocum figured that she was no innocent maid, but the last thing she had in mind was a tussle with a bloodthirsty Comanche. Slocum had seen the massacre at Six Deep Flats, and it was something to sicken the heart. Men battered and pierced with arrows like pincushions. The women raped and scalped. The Comanche was a specialist in revenge.

Slocum wondered if Maude had any idea of what she had escaped.

The sun was a blistering yellow disk in the noonday sky, and they were riding through brush country, when the sudden flash of white caught his eye. Lightning-quick, his gun barked and the jackrabbit dropped.

"Fresh meat for lunch," he said. He pan-fried the meat dark brown, and later poured steaming black coffee into two tin cups. His gut was beginning to feel grateful.

Until the coffee, Maude didn't say much. She seemed lost in her thoughts. "I suppose," she said finally, with a painful smile, "that if you hadn't come along, I'd be a wrecked woman by now."

"Could be." He sipped the hot coffee, thinking she was a damned sexy woman, and that he'd seen her naked body twice. It had left him horny as a goat.

"You always manage to be there when I need you, Slocum."

"It's a pleasure," He was thinking he needed a bit of her just now, but it couldn't be the sort of thing to tell her. Perhaps he could trade on her gratitude to get the lowdown on the Daltons.

"Did you know? Did you hear me when I broke camp this morning?" she asked.

"I knew."

Her eyes widened. "Why didn't you do something?"

"Like what?"

"Stop me."

"It's a free country," he said with a grim smile.

"Too free. I never figured on the Comanches."

He shrugged. "In this territory, you should figure on the worst happening, because it probably will."

She lifted the cup to her lips. "The worst almost happened to me. I can still smell the sweat of that redskin." She smiled slowly. "You saved me from a fate worse than death, Slocum."

He stared at her. "You can pay me off. It's easy. Tell me about that fracas between Dalton and Devlan."

He watched her eyes widen, then her mouth tightened. "I can't tell you any more than I have."

His green eyes were hard on her. "Was that story about the cattle straight?"

"No."

He waited, hoping now that she was putting out the truth, she would go on, but she didn't. It disappointed him. The Daltons had very specially hunted Devlan and killed him. He wanted to know why, not only because it might help him in his own trackdown of the Daltons, but because the more she held out, the more it intensified his curiosity. But she wouldn't talk, and he was not the man to twist it from her.

She'd been watching him and her mouth compressed as if with feeling. "I'm sorry, Slocum. It's something I can't talk about."

"Tell me this. If I knew, would it help me to track the Daltons?"

A veil passed over her hazel eyes. "No, it wouldn't help."

He felt sure she was lying, but there was nothing to be done.

The Daltons' tracks unmistakably went west. The land changed, turned grassy, with trees and rivulets. He saw a feeding herd of deer and a big-antlered stag, which raised its head to stare at them with hostile eyes. The screech of a hawk wrenched the air, and he watched it dive like a thunderbolt at its prey, hidden in the earth.

The afternoon waned, and purple clouds seemed to paste themselves around the peaks of the mountain. The sun turned into a giant globe of yellow-orange and slipped toward the horizon.

By tomorrow noon, Slocum figured, they would reach Sweetwater. He stopped at a rippling stream to let the horses drink, then turned them loose to graze. Then he dug a pit so their fire wouldn't be visible and they ate the leftover rabbit.

Slocum scarcely spoke. He was riled because she was close-mouthed, possibly a liar, and though he'd saved her hide twice, she still felt no need to help him about the Daltons.

In the purple twilight, he set up his bedroll near a cottonwood tree and settled in comfortably. Maude picked a spot twenty feet away.

Slocum watched the sky as it darkened, his mind on Sweetwater, where he expected to close in on the Daltons. They might pass through, of course, but if they did, they'd surely stop at the saloon to liquor up and maybe grab a woman. Sweetwater had its share of wicked ladies. He sighed: he sure could use one himself just now.

Then he heard her soft step, and though aware that it was Maude, his hand instinctively grabbed his gun, always near when he lay down at night.

"I don't think you'll need that," she said. The top two buttons of her shirt were loose, showing the rise of her breasts, and her shiny brown hair which she wore pinned back curled to her shoulders.

"You never know out here." He put the Colt down. His eyes squinted, wondering what was on her mind.

Her mouth twisted in a strange smile. "You're mad at me, aren't you, Slocum?"

He didn't smile. "A little."

She moved closer and then, to his surprise, sat next to him. "I can't give you what you want about the Daltons," she said slowly, her eyes big and dark. "But I can give you something else." And she leaned forward and kissed him.

Her action, entirely unexpected, jolted him, but it took only a moment for him to respond. He kissed her and his hands slipped into her shirt and he felt the creamy softness of her breasts. He'd seen them before, lusted for them, and now he could have them. He could have her. A nice exchange, he thought, grinning. Her body in the twilight was shockingly white. He reached for her nipples with his tongue, his hands moving over the silky flesh of her hips and buttocks. He stroked and kissed her, his hand moving between her thighs. While he stroked, his tongue played with her nipples. She sighed and her body strained toward him. His male flesh stood proud with passion. She bent to it, brought it against her lips, then brought him into the soft wonder of her mouth. He watched, delighted by the sensations, and after a time brought her back to the bedroll. Her thighs parted as he slid into her. She was velvety wet. He thrust all his maleness into her and she groaned softly. He moved, and she soon picked up his rhythm. He grasped her firm buttocks, plunging deep again and again. She moaned. He kept driving, his hands stroking her. Then, as his excitement increased, his drive became powerful, and he felt the swelling and spurt of passion. She moaned with pleasure as she too peaked. She lay in his arms, trembling. He, too, lay silent, in a trance.

The twilight deepened and all was quiet. Then he came up, and she smiled, looking at him, and abruptly came up, too, for a kiss. He heard the whoosh and the thump of the arrow as it buried itself into her back. His senses leaped alive searching for a sound or sight as his hand grabbed the Colt and the gun, as if it had a mind of its own, fired even before he clearly decided there was a target. But his instinct was right, for he heard a grunt and the crash of a body against the bushes. Then Slocum was on his stomach, crawling forward in the bushes, waiting for another clue while his mind raced. The second Comanche, of course. The damned pony had been picked up by the damned redskin, who had watched their coupling, then shot his arrow, hoping to spear the man and take the woman afterward.

Slocum found the Comanche sprawled in the bushes, not yet dead, a bullet in his gut. He was suffering, but he wouldn't make a sound before his enemy. Slocum watched as he reached into his belt for the knife and tried painfully to bring his arm back to throw it. Slocum's bullet crashed through his brain, and all consciousness of pain was gone. His eyes glared and his mouth fixed in death.

Slocum sat over Maude's grave. He didn't know her well, but the way she had died left him miserable. She had in a way saved his life by losing her own, because the arrow that hit her had been aimed at his heart.

A gentle wind rustled the grass, and he looked at the dark purple sky. Not too long before daylight. From a nearby grove of trees the scurry of a small animal sent the blackbirds into the air, flapping their wings frantically until they settled on the branch of a walnut tree. The pre-dawn silence around him felt eerie. He looked at the mound of the earth; she'd taken her secret, what she knew about the Daltons, down there. She knew something, all right; she was coupled with Devlan, so she couldn't be all that clean. Why else creep out of camp, if she hadn't been wrapped up with them? And she had done that even though Comanches were skulking about, risking a scalping.

She had had a short life; he hoped it had been merry. The morning wind touched his face, and he glanced to the ravine where he had dropped and covered the Comanche. Beams of light were starting to show in the eastern sky.

He swung over the big roan which had been standing patiently, as if aware of the feelings of his rider. But Slocum was thinking of the Comanches. Only a few hours ago, he'd seen their prints on the edge of the stream; there had been no way of knowing their paths would cross, that his gun would destroy them.

That's how it is, he thought as he nudged the roan forward. *You walk the earth one day, the next you're pushing up daisies.*

His mind went back to the War and the men he had seen die. Yes, he'd seen a lot of death and, up to now, except for a few knife and bullet scars, he'd survived. But you never knew, did you, when the bullet or the arrow that had your name on it would hit?

He pulled his Navy Colt to check it; it was clean and had five bullets. Did the Daltons have their names on two of them? You could ask the other way—did a Dalton bullet have his name on it? A lot was chance; all you could do was keep your eye peeled and try to think smart. The rest lay in the hands of that unpredictable lady—Lady Luck.

As he rode, he thought again of Maude coming up to kiss him because of her pleasure, and the way the smile on her face froze when the arrow hit her.

A wave of melancholy rolled over him.

The roan jogged toward Sweetwater.

From the gentle rise of the slope, astride the roan, he could see the town of Sweetwater baking in the heat of the Texas sun. The Daltons had taken this trail, and it was the one used by the stagecoach, which lay blood-smeared and empty back near Twin Fork, miles away.

Slocum's green eyes, keen and piercing, swept the land in front of him. That was his instinct, always to study what he would be riding into. Well-prepared is half the battle, he often told himself, and the trick was to keep your opponent from knowing you were prepared.

All he could see was a single cowboy slouched against a cottonwood, his horse grazing nearby. A siesta in the hot afternoon, maybe sleeping off the whiskey guzzled at the local saloon. Slocum scanned the land beyond and could see dust come up from some longhorns heading north, with cowboys riding herd.

Sweetwater, a fair-sized sprawl of two-story wooden houses, looked good to Slocum. He could use a good hot meal and a couple of blasts of whiskey to break his lousy mood, but that might come later. First the Daltons.

He felt ready to ride, but something flicked at his mind, and his eyes swept the terrain again, slowly this time. The slouched cowboy wore a flat black hat that seemed to come down over his eyes, but not quite. He wore a black vest and black chaps, and the way he slouched didn't look just right for a man trying to sleep off a drunk on a hot afternoon. Slocum shrugged; he might be misreading something routine. He nudged the roan forward, his eyes restless. Something bothered him, and he always paid attention to such feelings.

The hoofbeats of the roan seemed to wake the cowboy because he raised his head, stared, yawned, and, as Slocum came near, got slowly to his feet. He was lean and hard-looking, wore a Colt, black boots, and spurs.

"Howdy," he said.

Slocum nodded and pulled reins.

"The name is Gary, but I'm called Dakota." His eyes were like shiny black marbles, his face lean, broad-boned, hard-jawed, his hips slender, his shoulders broad. He didn't smile, and he looked dangerous.

Slocum swung off the roan, but said nothing, just mopped his brow.

Dakota didn't like the fact that Slocum didn't offer his name.

"I'm waiting for the stagecoach, mister. It's late . . . *very* late. You might know something about it, seeing that you come east."

Slocum spoke slowly. "The stagecoach got hit. Four dead."

Dakota's eyebrows went up, but the cold black eyes showed no feelings. "Four dead? I'm sorry to hear that." He studied Slocum. "Reckon you saw the bodies?"

Slocum nodded.

Dakota hitched his bullet-studded belt. "I'm particularly interested in a lady travellin' on that coach. It would grieve me to hear that she'd been hurt."

Slocum rubbed his chin. Would this fellow know Maude? Well, there was no telling who she knew; a woman of mystery.

"No," he said. "No dead woman there."

Dakota nodded as if not surprised. He studied Slocum, puzzled, as if he couldn't make up his mind about something.

"The lady's name was Maude McKay. Did you happen to meet up with her, while you was ridin'?" His voice was toneless.

Slocum stared at the lean, hard face, which had a knife scar on the left cheek. He wore a soiled red neckerchief, and his gun handle looked well polished, used plenty. He looked fast. Everything about him spelled gunfighter.

"What's your interest in this lady, can I ask?" Slocum said.

Dakota's black eyes looked flinty. "I'm interested in her, mister, and if you know something about her, it would go right with me if you tell it."

Slocum smiled grimly; if he did tell about Maude there would be no way to avoid a showdown with Dakota. He was not here by accident.

"She's dead," he said. "Took a Comanche arrow."

Dakota looked jolted; he hadn't expected that. "Dead?" He rubbed his jaw thoughtfully, then his hands dropped down to his waist. "How do you know it was Maude McKay who was dead?"

"She told me her name."

The muscles in Dakota's face grew hard. He frowned as if trying to figure Slocum out. He seemed puzzled to find no fear in Slocum.

"Did you know Maude McKay?" Slocum asked, his green eyes piercing and icy.

A long pause. "Yeah, I knew her, mister. A slut, a no-good, thieving bitch. It's too bad she died that easy."

The two men stared into each other's eyes, as if aware that in another minute one or the other or both would be dead.

"What's your name, mister?" Dakota's voice was harsh.

"Slocum. John Slocum."

There was silence, hard, agonized silence; then, as if the force of energy that seethed in the bodies of the two men disturbed the area, two crows abruptly flew out of the bushes. It was an unspoken signal and both men started. Slocum's hand was lightning fast and his bullet crashed into Dakota's chest. Dakota's own bullet hit the dirt as he reeled back. His face was in shock, as if this was the last thing in the world he expected. His astonished black eyes stared at Slocum as he started down in slow motion, down to his knees, his elbows, and he tried in agony to turn his gun up to fire again when suddenly his eyes went empty and he fell on his face.

Slocum took a deep breath and looked down. The Daltons again. They had sent Dakota out to intercept him, to find out about Maude, and to cut him down. They sent a fast gun, figuring he'd get what they wanted and then stop Slocum.

Slocum sighed. Dakota was young and like a lot of young killers, believed there was no one faster. But there was always a faster man, and Slocum hoped he'd know when he met that man, and hoped he'd be smart enough not to draw against him.

It was then he saw the lone horseman off to the southwest. He seemed frozen, almost a stone statue. Slocum tensed, cursing himself for being unaware of him, but nothing about the horseman looked threatening. In fact, he looked a bit old-timey. He'd seen the shootout, obviously, and when he realized Slocum was scrutinizing him, he made it his business to get out fast, racing his horse toward town.

Slocum pulled out a havana, lit it, glanced down at the dead Dakota, then put the roan into a slow trot. It didn't take long to reach town and he walked the roan up Main Street.

The town broiled under the hot sun, and Main Street was lively with cowboys, horsemen, and gunmen. It looked wide open, Slocum thought, where any cutthroat could work without fear of the law. As he rode past the Lone Star Hotel, an old man with a grizzled face sitting on the porch whittling a stick stared, then grinned, showing a mouthful of missing teeth. Slocum stopped at Casey's Livery and swung off the roan. Casey was brawny, with a freckled red face and sinewy arms. He had a hammer in his hand and he smiled.

"The name is Slocum. Put a pair of shoes on the front legs."

Casey nodded. "Mighty fine horseflesh." His professional eye went over the powerful roan.

"The best."

Casey's eyes were curious. "Passing through, Slocum?"

"It depends." He rubbed his chin. "I'm interested in the Daltons. Seen them?"

The blue eyes turned wary. "They been in town,

the Dalton bunch, but I wouldn't know where they are now."

"The Dalton bunch?" Slocum pushed his hat back, his piercing green eyes steady on the blacksmith. "Who is with the Daltons, would you say?"

"Don't you know?" The blacksmith still looked wary.

"I'd be much obliged if you'd tell me."

"The Dakota Kid, for one. I ain't seen Clem, just Red and Jessie."

Slocum nodded. He'd never see Clem again, and, as Slocum had figured, Dakota was one of them. It was a surprise to learn he was the Dakota Kid, a gunfighter with a big reputation. Well, he was fast, but not all that fast. A lot of fighters had bigger reputations than they deserved. Slocum examined the blacksmith. He looked square. "I wonder if you'd tell your burying man to go east out of town. He's got a customer out there." Slocum pulled out two dollars and held it to the blacksmith.

Casey took the money, his red face serious. "Who might it be, if I may ask?"

Slocum shrugged. "Called himself Dakota. He was a bit rambunctious."

Casey's eyes widened. "The Dakota Kid? You beat him in a draw?" His voice was incredulous.

Slocum's jaw hardened. "Well, I didn't bushwhack him."

Casey put down the hammer thoughtfully, looking embarrassed. "I'm sorry, Slocum. It's a shocker. Ain't nobody beat the Dakota Kid. He's got a rep long as your arm." He digested the idea and a new glint appeared in the blue eyes. "You gotta be greased lightning, Slocum."

Slocum's mouth was grim as he turned. "Sometimes a man's rep is better than his draw."

Casey grinned. "Well, well, the Dakota Kid. He won't be missed, Slocum. And I'll send Mr. Butler up there to collect the remains." He waved cheerfully to Slocum, who walked toward the saloon.

5

When he pushed the batwing doors of Big Jack's Saloon and Dance Hall, he was hit by the smell of whiskey and sweat. Men were drinking at the long bar and playing cards at the tables. Women in silky, tight-fitting dresses sat with the men. *No Daltons*. A big, tough-looking bouncer with a shotgun sat perched high on a chair against the wall. Slocum glanced at him and got a piercing look in return. He walked to the bar, and a tall, angular man behind it came toward him who had to be Big Jack; black hair, a cherubic smiling face, alert brown eyes that moved about carefully. He smiled at Slocum, taking in every inch, especially his gun.

"What's your pleasure, mister?"

"Whiskey."

Big Jack slapped a bottle and glass in front of

Slocum and stood there, his face friendly. Slocum belted the shot and Big Jack filled his glass again. In a courteous tone he asked, "Where yuh ridin' in from, mister?"

There was a big mirror behind the bar so that Slocum, facing Big Jack, could see the entire saloon.

"East," Slocum said.

"Comanches out there? See any signs?"

"Ran into a couple," Slocum said.

The cowboys who'd been talking nearby stopped and turned to listen.

"What happened, could a man ask?" Big Jack leaned his elbows on the bar.

"Well, I'm here." Slocum smiled. The tension at the bar loosened. "Just a couple of rambunctious Injuns. They won't give any trouble."

The men smiled, and Big Jack said, "Have one on the house, mister. Can I ask your name?"

"Slocum, John Slocum." In the mirror he saw a cowboy turn to look toward him, rise slowly, and come toward the bar. He was rosy-cheeked, fair-skinned, with a blond mustache grown, Slocum figured, to wipe out the tenderfoot look of his face. He wore buckskin with fringes and a Colt. He swaggered to Slocum then turned slowly to face him. The tenderfoot had pale yellow-brown eyes and an almost girlish mouth. Slocum's lips tightened. The kid spelled trouble. It was the damnedest thing the way trouble hit him hot and heavy these last days. What the hell was on this kid's mind? Even Big Jack could smell it, because he signalled the shotgun bouncer, who came to his feet.

The cowboy stood in front of Slocum, his hands

hanging loose. "Did you say your name was Slocum, mister?"

"That's it," His voice was benevolent. He had no interest in this yearling and wished he would go away. Slocum felt a flicker of irritation the way cowboys would come out of the woodwork, for one reason or another, to take potshots at him.

"My name, mister, is Jody Garrett, cousin kin to *Seth* Dalton."

Another Dalton, for God's sake. Was there no end of them? Slocum's jaw hardened.

"Cousin kin to Seth Dalton who you shot in Abilene," the cowboy drawled. "You'd be the same John Slocum. Am I correct?"

Everyone at the bar tensed, and some began to edge to the walls.

Slocum stared into the pale eyes. All the Daltons had these damned yellow-brown eyes. He smiled, and kept his voice friendly. "Seth was a fast but foolish cowboy who didn't like to lose in a card game. He made a mistake calling me a name and pulling his gun. I'm hoping you're smart enough *not* to make such a mistake, young Jody."

Jody's jaw was hard, and he looked as if he didn't think he would be making a mistake to draw against Slocum. He hitched his belt and looked tough.

Then Big Jack shook his head. "Jody, can I say something before things get out of hand?"

"I'm not sure you can say anything to stop that, Big Jack, but I'd be pleased to hear what's in your mind."

Big Jack nodded. "You know old Moose Withers? He just rode in and told me that he saw the Dakota

Kid in a showdown. The Kid is dead." He jerked his thumb at Slocum. "This is the gent who did it."

There was a stir of excitement in the bar, a murmur of voices.

The idea that Slocum had outdrawn the Dakota Kid seemed to hit Jody most unpleasantly. His eyes widened, his rosy skin started to pale, and his confidence seemed to ooze out of his skin.

Slocum spoke. "I've no quarrel with you, Jody. Let's just have a drink, and go our separate ways. That would suit me fine."

The bouncer shouldered his way in. "Yeah, Jody, we don't want to mess up the floor with any fightin'. So why don't you do that?"

Big Jack poured a couple of glasses. Jody cleared his throat and pulled his belt. "Well, when it comes down to it, I've got no quarrel with you, Mr. Slocum. The fact is I always thought Cousin Seth was somethin' of a fool, whose brain was as slow as his draw. Let's drink, then."

Everyone laughed, and they lifted their glasses.

Jody, after his drink and an uneasy scrutiny of Slocum, his size, and his gun, decided to make a graceful exit. So he nodded politely, and pulled his gunbelt, just to show he was tough and that if any cowboy questioned his guts he'd meet him halfway. Then he sauntered through the batwing doors into the harsh sunlight.

One thick-necked cowboy grunted, but the other men seemed to think Jody had acted sensibly. If Slocum had outgunned the Dakota Kid, which Moose Withers had seen with his own eyes, then it would be plain suicide for Jody to pull his pistol.

The mood in the bar got boisterous as the men

discussed the comic turnabout of Jody and the demise of the Dakota Kid, who had been something of a bully.

Slocum caught the eye of Big Jack, who leaned close over the bar. "Seen anything of Red Dalton or Jessie?" Slocum asked.

Big Jack's cherubic face went careful and his shrewd eyes gleamed. "It's not too smart around here to talk about Red Dalton, or Jessie, either."

"Why is that?"

"Red Dalton is a hard hombre and a smart gun. I'd hate to have him thinking bad about me."

Slocum's jaw clenched. "Well, I'm thinking bad about him."

Big Jack studied the green-eyed, hard-faced man in front of him. "I take it that Red put the Dakota Kid onto you. Is that it, Slocum?"

"I got a couple of grievances against him. So maybe if you tell me where he is I can talk to him about it."

Slocum watched the big barman rub his chin thoughtfully. "I figure you can take care of yourself, Slocum." He smiled. "Now the funny thing is Red was standing right where you are not that long ago. When Moose came in and told us that Dakota had been gunned down, Red didn't like it one damned bit. Dakota was the fast gun of that bunch. Red cursed up a storm, then went out, called Jessie after him."

Slocum's eyes narrowed. So they already knew about Dakota; that wasn't too good. He'd have to be extra careful. They might try to bushwhack him. The Daltons were the kind of men who'd gun a man in the back.

"Do you reckon they left town?"

Big Jack shook his head. "No way to reckon the way the Daltons move." He looked thoughtful, then grinned. "Tell you this: Jessie Dalton is one lovesick geezer. He's mighty smitten with one of our ladies. Mighty smitten. And I don't see a man like Jessie staying away from her."

Slocum glanced at the women, six of them, each in silky tight dresses, sitting with the men.

"Which is the lady?" Slocum asked.

Big Jack smiled. "She's upstairs, but she sings for the boys. She's due soon. A humdinger from San Antoine. Maybe you heard of her. Busty Bailey."

Slocum could scarcely believe his ears. *Busty!*

Just then a roar went up from the cowboys and Slocum turned sharply. Busty Bailey was coming down the stairs in a gleaming pink dress cut low to reveal a creamy wonder of a bosom, and the rest of her wasn't bad either. She stopped on the stairs to smile at her admirers, and the pianist, a thin black man with a cigar clamped in his teeth, hit "Dixie." Slocum's blood began to warm. He watched her come down, smiling broadly. She hadn't seen him yet. Her blonde hair was piled around her lovely oval face with its light blue eyes widely spaced, its high cheeks and full lips. In the yellow light, the skin of her face and rounded arms and the top of her deep bosom seemed to glow.

She began to belt it out. *"Oh, I wish I was in the land o' cotton."*

Slocum's Georgia heart began to beat in rhythm with the song. Busty Bailey was a Georgia peach herself; he'd met her six months ago in San Antoine. Thinking of it, he smiled. Then he thought of Jessie Dalton, a stinking coyote who had the balls to imagine himself good enough for Busty. It made his blood boil. The thought struck him that if ever there was bait to bring Jessie back to Sweetwater, it would be Busty. He watched as the cowboys, caught in the powerful rhythm of the song, some of them sons of the South, sang in whiskey-hoarse voices along with Busty.

Slocum's mind went back to Calhoun County, to his boyhood on the plantation. He sighed, thinking of the way things were, and that since the War he'd been a tumbleweed, wandering over the territories, a restless gun, searching for . . . what? He didn't know, but did it matter?

She was almost through the song when she saw him up against the bar. For a moment she stopped singing, then her smile broadened, and she picked up the song again. It made a couple of cowboys turn to look enviously at him.

Slocum just grinned and shrugged. He had met her in San Antoine three months ago and was fascinated: first by her figure, then by her Dixie songs, then her accent, in which he heard the familiar sounds of Georgia. They hit it off right fine, but a gunfight with one of her admirers, the rambunctious son of the town judge, had made discretion the better part of valor, and Slocum lit out at high speed when the judge mobilized a superior force against him. He gazed at her, singing now, and figured they had unfinished business, that if he played it right, he might get lucky, pick up where they had stopped, even manage to squeeze it in before he came to a showdown with the Daltons.

He put some money on the bar, took the bottle to an empty table, and watched Busty as she belted out two more heart-jerking songs. When she stopped, the cowboys yelled for more, but she just said, "This singin' has made my throat dry. I'll just sit a while and wet my whistle."

Some men grumbled but most were good-natured about it and watched her move to Slocum's table. Her full mouth spread in a grin. "John Slocum! You're a sight for sore eyes."

He stared at the swelling white breasts that had made her famous in the saloons of Texas. "And you're a feast for a man's eyes, Busty." He filled her whiskey glass and she tossed it off, presented the empty to him, and he filled it again. She sipped the drink.

"Guess you *are* thirsty," he said.

"Singing does it, and the sight of you doesn't hurt." Her clear blue eyes gazed at him. "I always wondered if they shot your butt off in San Antone."

He grinned. "I didn't stick around to give 'em a target. It meant leaving you . . ." He pulled out a havana. "But I figured if I ran away, I'd live to love another day." He stared with glazed eyes at her creamy breasts pushing outrageously against her dress.

She had to smile. "Slocum, you gotta move smart to stay alive in this territory. I suspect for a man like you it never was easy. What are you doing in Sweetwater?"

His lean, rugged face hardened. "It's the Daltons."

She frowned. "What about them?"

"I aim to blast their mangy butts." He stared at her. "I hope to hell you're not sweet on any of the Daltons. Find it hard to believe a woman like you would make such a mistake."

She patted her blonde hair. "The Daltons are an ornery bunch and mighty dangerous. You might be taking on more than even you can handle, Slocum.

The Dakota Kid is in with them. And he's a devil with a gun."

Slocum lit his havana. "We won't worry about him any more."

She stared at him as the meaning of the words hit her. "Well, if you dusted off Dakota, you did something nobody around here could do." She raised her glass, smiling. "You got a fast hand, Slocum, I always thought it. But I warn you about Red. He's a crafty dog, clever, tough, and mean."

He leaned forward. "Did you know Maude McKay or a man called Devlan?"

She shook her head. "Devlan sounds a bit familiar. I'm not sure."

His lips pressed tight. "What about Jessie Dalton?"

Her eyes squinted and she twisted the glass in her fingers. "Jessie is a hard man to handle. He thinks I'm the greatest thing that ever happened to Texas and he's been trying his damnedest to tumble me."

Slocum looked at her grimly. "And has he?"

"Not Jessie. I don't cotton to Jessie Dalton." She looked thoughtful. "But he's big, tough, and dangerous."

"I'll worry about him when the time comes," he said. "Meanwhile, you and me got some unfinished business. Right, Busty?"

Her eyes looked over his body slowly and she sighed. "To tell the truth, it was a misery to me when you streaked outa San Antone. I'd been looking forward to the pleasure of your company." She twisted a bit and those big bawdy breasts moved blissfully under her dress; it sent a shot of lust to his loins.

She leaned to him. "If I don't give these hungry cowboys a couple more songs, they'll tear the place apart. So, while I sing, you just go upstairs to the first room on the right. There's whiskey. I'll be up there quick as the shake of a squirrel's tail." She stood up and the curve of her body made him hungry. He watched her move toward the piano and the black pianist grinned, shifted the cigar in his mouth, and hit the keys. The cowboys yelled to show their pleasure.

She sang a wicked ditty about a wayward girl which gave the cowboys no end of joy, and while they stamped their feet, Slocum went quietly up the back stairs to her room. The bed looked feather-soft and large, there was whiskey and two shotglasses on a wooden table. He poured a drink, took it to the window. The sun was starting to swing west, but its glare hit the red dirt of Main Street hard. He looked down the street and on the porch of the Lone Star Hotel, perched on a rocker, Jody sat, rocking gently and staring into space.

Slocum didn't care for that. Jody, when you came down to it, welshed on a showdown, and there were two ways to handle that. One was to ride off and thank your stars that your skin was still whole. The other was to find a chair and brood about it. Brood that your nerve was now busted, that you'd be tagged with a yellow streak. Jody looked like a brooding man. What the hell would he do?

Down below, the singing had stopped, and Slocum turned when he heard footsteps. It was Busty, and she shut the door behind her with an impish smile. She looked so pink, curvaceous, and sexy that the room seemed to glow with her presence. She walked to the table, poured a shot of whiskey, and gulped it, throwing her head back. Her swelling breasts strained against the satin dress, and it astonished him that they didn't break the seams and pop out.

"Do you remember where we were in San Antone," he said, "when they started to break down the door?" He moved close to her and put his hands on her rounded white arms. "I was kissing you, like this." He bent and kissed her full red lips. "Then," he went on, "that damned pounding on the door, and though I was primed like a sex-starved stallion, I had to jump out the window to get away."

She smiled at the memory. "Yes, Slocum, and you left behind a very disappointed lady."

He leaned down, looked into her blue eyes that seemed to be smoldering. He pressed her, felt her magnificent breasts against his chest, and his body seemed to go on fire.

He kissed her again, and his hands slipped over her breasts and he felt their fullness and silkiness. He reached behind to unfasten her buttons and pulled at the dress and the globes came out, big beautifully shaped, with fat pink nipples. He leaned down to them, smoothed them against his lips, nuzzled them, let his tongue caress them, and buried his face between the beautiful mounds. Her breath started to come fast. He pulled away, and they undressed at furious speed. He stared at her body, the slightly rounded belly, the curving womanly hips, slender waist, fine strong legs, and the blonde hair that hardly hid the pouting red lips between her thighs.

Her eyes were wide as she looked at his maleness in its state of frantic tension.

He came close to her again, put his mouth to her nipple and his finger down to the pouting lips. She was velvety wet, and he stroked the tender spot, over and over, his mouth loving her breasts, his other hand caressing her rounded buttocks. He played this way for a time, and she stiffened as the pulsations raced through her body. Then she slipped to her knees, put his swollen excitement against her face, against her lips, brushing her mouth over it, then opening her mouth to take it into her liquid warmth. She cupped him and her mouth moved with marvelous skill and he, looking down, felt pleasure and wonder at her insatiable appetite.

Then he pulled her up, brought her to the bed, turned her so that she leaned over, and he slipped past her buttocks into her. She was warm and tight and she snuggled, sliding on him smoothly.

He leaned forward to hold her dangling breasts and moved in rhythm. His hands caressed her buttocks and her body, and after a while he turned her and she lay on her back and he speared her to the bed, holding her buttocks. Each stroke gave her excruciating pleasure; her hips rose to meet his rhythm, and his excitement mounted, his thrusts became frantic, then he felt the great swelling and spurting. A smothered gasp came from her as her body went into its own pulsations of pleasure. She held him tightly and breathed his name.

They fell back on the bed, spent.

After they dressed, she turned and said, "Slocum, you spoil me for other men."

He grinned. "I try to do my best."

She laughed and threw a pillow at him. Then he heard soft footsteps on the stairs and his gun was out. The door opened and there stood Jessie Dalton.

6

Jessie Dalton's gun was in its holster, and he just stood there staring, his yellow eyes baleful with hate. He was big, almost as big as Red Dalton, but he had black hair, with a lean, tight-skinned face, jutting cheekbones, a square chin, and a thick, muscular neck. He was big-chested, had big biceps and thick, knobby fingers. He looked at the bed, and his mouth twisted venomously.

Then he stared at Busty. "I don't know how you can bear to be with someone like him, Miss Bailey. But you have made a bad mistake. And I'm going to take him off your hands."

Slocum smiled, his eyes icy. "I think, Busty, I could put a bullet right in the middle of his forehead from here. But I don't want this stinkin' hyena's blood messing up your room."

Jessie's lips twisted scornfully. "I wouldn't put it past you to shoot a man who hasn't drawn his gun. But I didn't come up here to spill your blood in front of a woman. It'll be sundown shortly. And if you got any guts, you'll meet me out there for a showdown. I'll pay you back for the slimy way you killed Clem and Seth."

Slocum shook his head. "You got it all wrong, Dalton. You're the slime around here. I'll see you out there." He stroked his chin. "Where's Red?"

"He's outa town. Didn't know you'd be here. If he did, he'd have blasted you before you came up here to try and take advantage of this woman."

"You're stupid, like all the Daltons," Slocum drawled. "Now just ease outa here careful-like; you're stinking up the room."

Jessie's mouth curled and he backstepped slowly. His yellow eyes didn't leave Slocum until he was about to shut the door and then they swung over to Busty. The sight of all that swelling femininity touched his rascal heart, for he smiled and blew her a kiss, then shut the door.

Slocum grinned. "He's madly in love with you."

She fluffed her hair. "I don't wish to sound conceited but there are thirty cowboys downstairs who seem to have that disease." She stared hard at him. "What is it you got against the Daltons? Clem and Seth. You shot them. Now you aim to get Jessie. Are you trying to wipe out all the Daltons?"

He shrugged. "The Daltons wanted to wipe *me* out. First that stupid Seth, in Abilene, accused me of cheating, because *he* couldn't play poker, and pulled his gun. Then the Daltons came after me, forced me to bust a virgin and put me in the power of her father, who has a habit of castrating men who even look at his daughter." He stood up. "I don't cotton to that idea."

She looked startled. "Castrate? You? That'd be the crime of the year." She thought for a moment, then a slow smile twisted her "It was a neat scheme for revenge, wasn't it? The Daltons are not stupid. They're ornery, and God knows what wicked things they've done. But they're not stupid, and you'd be smart not to underestimate them."

He walked to the window and looked out. The sky already had an orange blush as the sun started down.

"They're smart when it comes to killing, but otherwise they're stupid," Slocum said, and he checked his gun.

Busty's pretty lips pressed tightly. "All this fightin'. It's bad to give your heart to anyone in this territory. You love him one day, he's liable to turn up his toes the next."

He came close and pressed against her beautiful bosom. "Busty, if Jessie is a faster gun, I can't think of a better way to go out than with a memory like this." He kissed her and she held him tightly, then he walked to the door, held the knob. But he heard something, his instincts screamed, and he leaped aside as two bullets ripped through the door slats. His gun, already in hand, spit fire at the door, and he heard the thud of a body collide with the floor. Gun at the ready, he jerked the door open, expecting to see Jessie, but it wasn't Jessie. Jody Garrett, with two bloody holes in his chest, slumped against the wall.

He could scarcely breathe, but he looked up at Slocum and spoke painfully. "That backdown...I couldn't live with it, Slocum. And...I don't deserve to live . . . sneaking like this. It . . . it was Jessie . . . Jessie." His voice faded. "I'm sorry," he whispered, and he died.

"I'm sorry, too, Jody," Slocum said grimly.

Later, in the corner of the saloon, Slocum sat nursing a drink, waiting for the sky to turn bloody, because he wanted in the worst way to get Jessie Dalton. It didn't take much to figure that it had been Jessie who put the bug in Jody's ear, fed Jody's burning need to square himself, even suggested how to do it, through the door. It was a pity, Slocum thought, that the skunk behind the door hadn't been Jessie, but he'd try his damnedest to take care of Jessie. The sky was beginning to get bloody and in minutes Jessie would be walking out there. Before the sun went down this day, either Jessie or Slocum would be dead.

Just then Busty who, since Jody's botched sneak attack, had been serious-faced, sat next to him. One of Jody's bullets in that room had whistled past her head, and she was feeling no charity for the Daltons.

"Slocum, you asked me if I knew about Devlan. It's come back to me. Still interested?"

Slocum turned to her. "Yeah, I'm interested."

"His name came up some weeks ago with one of the cowboys at the bar telling about a bank job in Fort Worth. I remember he named Devlan as a robber. The name stuck because I knew someone in Georgia name of Devlan."

Slocum stared at her. Devlan a bank robber? What did that mean? Maude had been tied up with Devlan, so she must have known about the bank job. Could that explain why she was so tight about Devlan? And the Daltons? They had run Devlan to ground, hadn't they? Somehow they knew he had done the bank job and were going to pin his ears back until he told where he'd cached the money. Did Maude know, and could that be why she'd tried to slip out of the camp? It explained something. Now the secret of that bank money was buried with Devlan and Maude.

He raised the glass to his lips and looked out the door. A bloody sky was starting. Sundown. He smiled. If you thought about it, this whole bank deal didn't matter a fig if he caught a bullet from Jessie. But it explained a couple of things: why the Daltons chased the stagecoach, why they nailed Devlan, and Maude's sneak-out. He liked it when puzzles were solved.

Now it was time to get on that street.

At the bar, the men watched him. Busty watched him. The card players watched him. Word of a showdown always got out. The town knew. The drama of life and death on a street in a godforsaken town seemed to be the one entertainment left to cowboys in the territory.

He pushed out of the chair. The saloon went silent. He glanced at Busty; her eyes were fearful. Women felt fear at the thought of death. Maybe they hated to see human life killed since they gave birth to it. He shook his head; hell of a time to think such thoughts.

He checked his gun, put it back in his holster. As he walked to the doors, he glanced at Big Jack behind the bar. He was untying his apron, making ready to see the fun from the porch. The men were gulping their drinks. They'd all heard that Slocum had dusted off the Dakota Kid, and some of them couldn't help wondering if it had been a fluke, if Slocum had tricked Dakota. Now, from the porch of the saloon, they would see with their own eyes how good Slocum was.

Jessie Dalton had a fearsome rep, and a lot of cowboys were pushing daisies because of his gun.

Slocum stepped out into the empty street. The sky was a flame of crimson and shone in the windows.

His body mobilized, his senses alert, Slocum walked slowly down the center of the street.

A queer hush lay over the town. Not a dog barked, not a bird flew, and the sun stuck on the horizon, as if nature knew the street held the smell of death, and watched.

At the far end of the street opposite the bar, the door of a two-story house opened and Jessie came through it, big and bulky in his black shirt, faded black chaps, his gunbelt hung low, his big hands hanging near his black-handled gun.

He was smiling, and to Slocum he looked almost cocky, as if he felt himself indestructible, that he expected Slocum would shortly bite the dust.

As they walked toward each other, Slocum felt his nerves strain, felt the heat of the sun-baked street, felt eyes watching from everywhere.

Jessie kept coming, his smile fixed, as if painted on. They were about forty feet apart.

Then Jessie stopped.

Slocum stopped.

He saw the sweat on Jessie's brow and knew that, in spite of the smirk, Jessie felt fear.

Everything along the street held its breath.

Jessie went for his gun. Just as he got it from the holster, the sound of gunfire punched the silence of the street.

A bullet from somewhere struck glass.

A bullet ripped the flesh of Slocum's shoulder.

A bloody rose appeared on the side of Jessie's head.

Slocum dived flat, crawled toward the side of a house for cover. His mind worked like lightning. He'd heard three shots: his, which hit Jessie, and two others, one that hit a window, one that came from that window, which hit his left arm.

It had been an ambush, and even as he scrambled to the side of the house for cover, he figured out what had happened. A gunman in the window of the last house had given Jessie backup to make sure he won the showdown. But someone, aware of the ambush, had fired at the gunman to spoil it. Now, who in hell did it?

He glanced at Jessie, lying flat like a dead log, his gun just out of its holster, still unfired. Then he stared at the broken window on the second story, where Jessie's backup gunman might be crouched even now for another shot. For a fleeting moment he wondered about the man who'd saved his life, where he was perched, but time was too short; he could still get his brains shot out, he had to move. Slowly he crawled on elbow and knees, sticking for cover close to the house. The street was empty and silent; nothing moved. The blood red of the sky seemed to get bloodier.

Slocum crawled a few feet, waited.

Then came the sound of hooves hitting the earth. He peered out but could see nothing. Someone was running a horse hell-bent to get out of town. Could it be the gunman? He could have dropped from the window in back of the house to a waiting horse. Slocum moved fast, hugging the walls for cover, till he reached the break in the street, and rushed through it. Then he saw the big cowboy spurring his horse unmercifully, too far for a bullet, but not too far to be recognized: Red Dalton.

Slocum gritted his teeth. The Daltons never in their lives fought fair. They always played with a stacked deck.

He started for his horse. It would be nice to know who had befriended him, saved him, and, if he survived, he'd come back to find out; but just now one thing was on his mind: Red Dalton. In the next twenty-four hours either Red or he would be dead.

7

Slocum raced the roan hard, staying on the track of Red, tracks that went west.

The sun, it seemed, had hung on the horizon, as if waiting for the bloody show on the street in Sweetwater to go on. Then it started down.

Red had raced through brush country, through prickly pear, pin oak, and juniper, and Slocum realized that if a man rode carefully, he could stay under cover a lot of the time. A man who picked country like this for running had to know what he was doing.

The dark came down fast now, and he was forced to make camp, which he did near a spring.

He let the roan drink, set his bedroll in a thick cluster of bushes. Red Dalton was a man who favored ambush, and it would be stupid to give him a target for a second time today. He made no fire, ate beef jerky, drank water from the spring, and put his gun near his hand as he settled down in the bedroll.

The moon came up, big and yellow, light enough for a creeping gunman to do his dirty work. Still, Slocum felt easy this night. Red had to be feeling rotten, lowdown, might even be mourning Jessie. If Red was human, and Slocum was willing to allow him that, he had to be suffering from the loss of his kin, even face the idea that he was the last of the Daltons. If he knew that the gunman who wiped out his kin was hot on his trail, he wouldn't be sleeping good.

Slocum put his hands behind his head and watched the moon climb. Maybe Red didn't give a damn about anything but his own skin and did no mourning for anyone. Still, he must want revenge. That would be his style: revenge for blood. Busty had warned him that Red was tricky. A hyena of a man she had said. It had to be Red behind the ambush in Sweetwater. It was Red who figured it would be cute revenge to get Slocum to "bust" Charity, and put his balls under O'Rourke's hammer. Red was the leader of the bunch. He called the shots, and he was the one Dalton still riding, still scheming.

That was why, as long as Red Dalton lived, Slocum felt he couldn't sleep easy.

Again Slocum wondered who had saved his hide by firing at Red. He had a nick in his upper left arm; not serious, it had bled a bit.

He listened to the night sounds, the doleful wail of the coyotes, the wild flutter of a blackbird's wings, the scrabble of field mice. He could smell juniper, and suddenly he felt it was a beautiful June night, a good time to be alive. Strangely, the image of Jessie sprawled on the dust of Main Street came back to his mind.

Now heaviness crept over his eyelids. It had been a rough day. Busty, Jody, Jessie. What would tomorrow bring? he wondered, slipping into the kind of sleep when one part of his mind seemed to be listening to the sounds of night, deciphering them for danger.

The night slipped away, and he opened his eyes to the glow of dawn, the sweet smell of grass. He made a fire and boiled coffee, pulled a biscuit from his saddlebag. The coffee warmed his gut and as he drank he watched the glow drain from the sky. It shaped up like a scorcher. He filled two canteens, patted the roan, checked its hooves for burrs. The chestnut brown of the roan's neck gleamed beautifully, and Slocum, looking at the big glowing eyes of the horse, felt a great rush of affection. The roan seemed to feel it, for he nuzzled roughly against Slocum's chest. It came to Slocum, as he swung over the saddle, that sometimes he felt more for the roan than for a lot of human beings he'd known.

He picked up Red's tracks, riding though flat dusty land.

Red had pushed his horse at a hard pace. Slocum soon realized, to his astonishment, that Red had been riding all night, aiming to put a lot of land between them. At least that was how Slocum figured it. Dalton seemed to be riding toward Dawson.

As he expected, the day went hot as the sun climbed, and after a time his body felt sticky, and the roan's coat became dusty, wet with sweat. Slocum was glad when he found a small stream; the roan stepped into it to cool down as he drank. Slocum peeled off his clothes and jumped into the crystal clear water to refresh his sweltering body. Afterward, as he rode, the land turned wooded and rocky and late in the afternoon he climbed some piled-up boulders and studied the country. He came alert at the slight glitter on the trail behind him. His piercing green eyes fixed on it steadily, but he couldn't figure it. Could it be a trick of the sun on a shiny stone, or was it someone on his track? He rubbed his chin. It couldn't be Red; there'd be no way he could have circled the great spread of ridges.

Then he saw movement. Someone on his tail. Comanche? One of the Dalton bunch out for revenge? Maybe another Dalton; there seemed no end of them. He'd make sure; ride a couple of miles.

He had no doubt when he checked again that someone was cutting his trail, and his jaw clenched. That someone had to be hostile. Slocum rode slowly and then positioned himself not far from a spring. On a scorcher of a day like this the horseman wouldn't bypass it; he'd need water for his horse.

He left the roan in a dense thicket and doubled back, staying behind brush and rock. Once he caught a glimpse of the horseman, a slender, easy-riding cowboy in a Stetson who moved steadily. And, as he expected, the rider stopped to let his horse drink. Softly, Slocum moved through brush until he got behind the cowboy. He stepped out, his gun pointing.

"Don't move." The cowboy froze. "Now lift your gun carefully and drop it." The cowboy did that. He looked young, slender, quick. "Now, mister, you been riding my tail. Why? You better have good reason."

The cowboy turned sharply and Slocum's eyes widened with shock. It was Charity O'Rourke in faded jeans and a Stetson.

He stared into her soft cornflower-blue eyes and the jolt of seeing her took almost a minute to wear off. A slow smile came to the pretty face. She wore a checked blue shirt and tight faded jeans that hugged the graceful spread of her hips. Only because he'd expected the horseman to be a cowboy on a trail of revenge had he missed the female curve of her body. He was so amazed that he said stupidly, "Is it you, Charity?"

"None other."

He tried to think how in hell she had got here. "What in blazes arc you doing here?" he asked.

"After you," she said matter-of-factly. "I'm really after Red Dalton, but since you are, too, our trails have come together."

She leaned to the spring, cupped water in her palms, and sipped it. He watched, speechless.

She turned, took her hat off, and shook her blonde hair. It shone golden in the sun and fell to her shoulders. "I've been tailing you a long time, John Slocum. Just came outa Sweetwater, hot after you."

"You been tailing me since Twin Fork?" he said disbelievingly.

She shook her head. "Oh, I knew you were headed for Sweetwater."

"How'd you know?"

"Because the Daltons were at Sweetwater." She smiled prettily. She sat on a small boulder, folded her hands round a knee, enjoying his astonishment. "It was lucky for you that I got to Sweetwater when I did."

Thoughts spun in his head, but that remark stopped him cold. "Lucky? What do you mean?"

A secret smile. "I mean...well, you know it was Red Dalton who shot at you. Meant to shoot you down like a dog from an upstairs window?"

"Yeah, I knew that." He touched his bandaged arm.

She looked concerned. "He did hit you, after all."

"A scratch." He stared at her. "Just keep talking."

"Who do you suppose shot at *him?*"

His eyes widened.

She nodded. "Too bad I missed, but it jarred him some, spoilt his aim." She smoothed her hair. "I was coming out of the livery, just after reaching town. I saw Red and Jessie go into the last house. I crept into the empty barn opposite, at the end of the street which gave a good view. Saw Red at the window with his gun, Jessie walking toward you. You know the rest."

Slocum shook his head, amazed. "Little lady, I'm sure glad you decided to track me."

She grinned. "I'm glad, too. Too bad I missed Red, that was the main thing. To pay him off. I'm still after him. And, since you are, too, we can join forces." She gave him a sly smile.

He gritted his teeth. What in hell could he do about this filly? She had to be crazy to think he'd let her ride with him. So far she'd been lucky. She could have run into a drifter or a Comanche. Still, she seemed able to handle a gun and a horse. How else could she have trailed him or shot at Red? And how did she get away from her old man, O'Rourke, who seemed to put such a high price on her purity? And the main question: could she keep up the pace? To nail Red Dalton, he'd have to travel fast and hard. He looked at her gelding. She'd bragged on it, he remembered. It did have a powerful chest and good legs.

But all this was crazy. He looked at her. Her chin set hard.

"Don't think, John Slocum, that you can send me packing. Don't think it for a second. I'm here to do a job. I aim to track down Red Dalton and put a bullet in his rotten heart. I'd like to have your help, but if you won't help, then I'll do it myself."

He almost had to laugh. She was a fawn, graceful, young, feminine, and she was making sounds like a mountain lion. What should he do? The truth was he couldn't send her back alone in this wild territory. She might run out of luck, and run into a lowdown drifter just craving for a filly like her.

So he had her on his hands, whether he wanted her or not. After all, he did owe her something. He'd be as dead as Jessie right now if she hadn't been at the shootout.

"Come," he said, "I gotta pick up my horse."

A brilliant smile. "You won't be sorry, John Slocum. You're going to need my help."

He growled. "You're gonna be an albatross around my neck. I'll worry about you when I need to worry about Red Dalton."

She pushed her hair under the Stetson, put her foot in the stirrup, and swung light over her gelding. "I'll be no trouble, Slocum. You'll be glad I'm here. And don't forget, it's me that has the biggest grievance against Red Dalton. It's me that owes him a bullet in the heart."

She gave him a sly, sidelong glance. "Also, you'll need me to put in a good word for you, Slocum. My dad's coming with a posse." She started her horse. "They're after me, after you, and after Red Dalton." She smiled cheerfully.

He stared at her, thunderstruck.

He grabbed the reins of her gelding and pulled hard. His voice sounded harsh. "Are you telling me that your father is coming after you and me *with a posse?*"

"He's coming after Dalton, too," she said casually.

Something in his face got to her, because she flushed. Then shrugged. "Don't blame me. He was going after Red Dalton. Then you escaped. He felt he had unfinished business with you. When I ran off, that clinched everything. He's got blood in his eyes."

Slocum looked at the creamy smoothness of her face, the soft blue of her eyes, the innocence of her youth. He gritted his teeth, "It's hard to believe, looking at you, but why do you always spell a mess of trouble every time I see you?"

"Who, me?" she said with wide open eyes, "I was just minding my own business when some mangy dog called Red Dalton grabbed me and threw me to you to eat alive." There was almost a glint of humor in those soft blue eyes. "I'm just trying to pay back the dog that done me wrong."

He thought about it. He, too, was trying to do that, so he couldn't fault her. But why wasn't she home, like good little girls were supposed to be? "It's man's business you're trying to do, Charity."

Her face hardened, the innocence vanished. "A bullet's got no sex," she said.

He looked at the great soaring mountain, where clouds hung like great bunches of cotton round its peaks.

Then he started toward the roan. Charity followed on the gelding. His mind worked on the piece of dynamite she'd dropped so quietly. O'Rourke and a posse thundering down the trail, out to nail his hide to a post. He remembered O'Rourke's big, beefy face, distorted with rage when he learned what happened to his daughter. He didn't look like a man who diddled around. He had clipped the balls of the youngest Dalton for molesting Charity. Such a man wouldn't stop for breath to avenge the honor of his daughter.

So now he was in a crunch; Red Dalton in front and five bloody-eyed gunmen behind. He in the middle, saddled with Charity. He was trying to concentrate on Red Dalton, to track and destroy him, but how could he do that with Charity hanging on like a ball and chain and O'Rourke breathing fire behind him? To be smart, he should ride like a hellbound, force Red into a showdown, and, if he survived, break for New Mexico, leaving the pack of them behind. But could he do that? Charity, in spite of her wild ideas, had put herself in his protection. And *he* just didn't run. So he had to take her, and hope that when they closed on Red, somehow he could drop her and take Red on alone.

Slocum smiled; if you thought about it, the trackdown might be more fun with Charity trotting alongside. Then he bit his lip. There could be no thought of snuggling with that young lady. He'd done it the first time under the compulsion of the Daltons' guns. He had no right to touch her again.

The pleasures of her body came to his mind with such a rush that he cursed silently. Not only would he be fighting Red Dalton, but fighting himself, his desires. It had been a dirty trick for Charity to come down on him like this, but that was how the dice fell, and Slocum was not one to quarrel with fate.

He'd try one more time to make her see the light. He stopped.

"My advice to you, Charity, is to wheel around right here and join your father." He looked at her lovely young face and added, "And spend some time growing up."

Her jaw hardened. "I'm grown up, John Slocum. And you're wasting your breath. Why don't you get on your horse, and let's trackdown that yellow-belly Dalton." Her blue eyes glinted with steel. Slocum sighed. She sounded like a chip off her father.

"All right," he said, stern-faced. "It's not going to be a party out there. Anything can happen. And whatever happens, I don't want to hear one word of complaint outa you."

She smiled a secret smile, as if she'd won a victory, and he felt like spanking her young butt.

8

It was easy to stay on Dalton's tracks because the prints of his big black had a sharp crack in the right back hoof. Slocum could read Dalton's movements clear as a book: when he raced, when he dawdled, when he stopped to study the terrain for signs of danger. Everything Dalton did showed judgment, Slocum thought: the trails he picked, the places he camped; they were all strategic. Riding most of the first night to get a big jump had also been a smart move. He kept riding west, and it looked like Dawson, but he might turn anytime and see his tracker.

Two trackers now, Slocum thought grimly, glancing at Charity. She rode nicely, her back erect, her butt planted firmly in the saddle, her breasts pushing against her checked shirt. She had a sharply etched profile, straight nose, finely curved lips, and under her small Stetson, the wisp of her golden hair curled against her cheek. Not quite the bloodthirsty hunter needed to track down a desperado like Red Dalton, Slocum thought, but a pretty girl. He remembered her body, all curves, and the white creamy skin, the golden hair between her thighs—a body new to sex and to pleasure.

He shook his head to rid it of dangerous pictures and scolded himself for being stupid. He couldn't touch her again; it wouldn't be right. And why was he dreaming about sex when he should be concentrating? This was bad country where sudden death could spit from anywhere. So, just as he had feared, Charity was turning out to be a distraction—which could get them killed.

He clamped his teeth and his eyes searched the land, reading nature for the slightest clue that might betray the presence of man.

The trail took them through a green valley spotted with golden dandelions, then through groves of cottonwoods. A good place to be bushwhacked; it kept Slocum on edge.

The sun began to descend, and in the distance the cluster of clouds round the peaks of the mountain turned purple. It took some time until he found a good campsite near a great oak. He climbed a high rock to study the surrounding land. No sign of Red, and because of the quick gathering dusk he could scarcely see anything behind him on the trail. He should have struck camp earlier, he thought, and cursed his carelessness. He always made a clear point of camping before the shadows. Now the shadows behind him were impenetrable, and it left him uneasy.

He rubbed down the horses, put them to graze

nearby, then dug the ground for a deep-pitted fire. They ate a pheasant he had shot earlier. As they ate, the sun went down, then the dark came, and silver bits exploded in the heavens.

He felt a glow, which came from a loaded stomach; it almost made him feel kindly to Charity who, just being there, kept him on edge. Though she had pushed herself into this trackdown, he still felt responsible for her.

"Any idea how far back that posse would be?" he asked.

She shrugged. "About twenty-four hours."

"And they're coming?"

She nodded. "Come hell or high water. You don't know my dad."

His voice chilled. "I'd rather not know him." He scattered dirt over the fire. "Does he know you've come after me?"

She smiled. "Oh, yes, and I told him he was all wrong about you. That you were a Southern gentleman."

Slocum smiled. "More Southern than gentleman. What'd he say?"

She grinned. "I'm too ladylike to repeat it. He thinks you took advantage of me." Her smile broadened. "That you raped a virgin and deserved to be skewered like a coyote."

"He's a nice daddy," said Slocum. "Reminds me of a rattlesnake on my plantation in Georgia."

"You shouldn't cuss out my daddy. He just cares about his only child, his darling daughter." She looked at him archly. "Course, you *could* make an honest woman of me."

He glared at her. "You're just outa the crib, Charity. I'm not baby stealing yet."

Her blue eyes glinted fire. "I saved your hide in Sweetwater, Mr. Slocum. That wasn't a baby shooting that gun."

He sighed. "You're right, and I apologize. Let's forget about your daddy. It's painful to think of him. It's Red I'm after. I figure he's going to Dawson."

She shrugged.

"You got a different idea?" His tone was sarcastic.

"He might be going for the bank money," she said.

He came alert. "What's that? What do you know about it?"

Her eyebrows went up and she looked superior. "All the big news in Texas gets to the O'Rourke ranch, Slocum. The Dalton bunch robbed the bank in Fort Worth. Did you know that?"

He stared at her, astonished. All he knew was what Busty had told him, that Devlan had been in the robbery at Fort Worth. "What about it?" he demanded.

"It's just that the Daltons didn't end up with the money."

"What do you mean?" He thought about it. "What do you know about Maude McKay?"

She looked queerly at him. Was it something in his tone? Then she nodded. "That's it, Maude McKay and Scotty Devlan were a pair. When the bunch were forced to split after the robbery, Maude and Devlan were carrying the money and they scooted off somewhere. The Daltons have been trackin' them. I heard they finally caught up." She smiled. "You may think that Red Dalton is running from you. I don't think he'd run from a fight. I reckon he's running somewhere else."

Slocum listened, amazed. Charity lived on the

O'Rourke ranch, and Sean O'Rourke, one of the most powerful men in Texas, would receive news like the bank job in Forth Worth. And Charity, sitting in the middle of it, would pick up such news.

So now the Daltons' movements made sense. Why they pursured the stagecoach, why they kicked Devlan around, why they used Maude as bait. Was Red running away or running to something? Well, it didn't matter; he'd stick with Red Dalton's tracks to the bitter end.

Charity had an odd expression. "Did you meet up with Maude McKay?" she asked.

"Yes, I met up with her." His voice was grim as he thought of how Maude caught the arrow.

"How'd that happen?"

"I saved her hide during the stagecoach shootout at Twin Oak."

She looked thoughtful. "So *you* shot Clem Dalton, that right?"

He nodded, watching her.

"I been told," she drawled, "that Maude was a good-looking woman."

"Almost as good-looking as you, Charity."

Her blue eyes glinted; she was something of a spitfire. *"Almost.* I suppose you two did *things."*

"Did what things, Charity?"

"The things you did to me."

He could scarcely repress a smile. This was jealousy time. "I did those things to you because I had guns pointing at me."

She looked at him, her teeth showing. "Did it because you were afraid to die."

That was a miserable remark; it was she who had persuaded him!

"Everyone's afraid to die, Charity," he said simply.

Her lip curled with contempt. "I thought you were a real man, a Texas man. Texas men aren't afraid."

He laughed. "In that case, find yourself one of these brave Texas men and leave me in peace."

Her lips drew back in anger, showing white teeth. "I'm disappointed in you, Mr. Slocum. Very disappointed." She turned away. "I hope we get Red Dalton tomorrow so I don't have to spend another moment with you."

He shrugged. "To tell the truth, Charity, nothing frightens me more than being near you. Because where you go, your dad follows. And he's got four guns with him and some nasty ideas about me."

Her lips firmed. "Well, I don't want you hurt on my account. After we get Red Dalton, you just go on your way."

"Sounds good to me, Miss Charity," He said formally, and took his bedroll toward one of the rocks.

He left her near the oak trunk to give plenty of room for her modesty, and put his bedroll against a boulder at least thirty yards away. The moonlight sifted through a heavy layer of clouds, and as he lay back on the bedroll, Slocum put his gun near his right hand and stretched, feeling the ache in his muscles from a long day's riding. He glanced at the trunk where Charity lay, turning and probably smoldering because of his harsh words. He felt a touch of regret that he'd dug his spurs so hard into her; though she was a spitfire, there was no call to do that. But when she said, "You could make an honest woman of me," it jolted him. Sounded like a shotgun coupling. He'd been forced to screw her because of Red Dalton's gun. And now she seemed to be suggesting he marry her. Chances were, he thought, turning sleepily on his side, the last man O'Rourke would think fit for his little girl would be a skunk like Slocum.

So thinking, he drifted into sleep.

When he opened his eyes he figured only minutes had passed until he saw the moon clear and far to the west. Must be three hours at least. Then he felt his nerves crawling; it meant danger, and damned close; he never ignored his intuition. Lightning-fast, his hand had the gun and he started up. Then came the voice.

"Drop the gun, Slocum."

He could scarcely believe his ears—that voice! He lifted himself on his elbow, his gun pointing, ready to fire.

"Drop the gun or *she* gets it, Slocum."

Then he saw them: Charity, her mouth covered by the hand of the big cowboy who, using her body as a shield, stood behind her, holding his gun against her head.

Jessie.

Alive! A bandage showed white under his hat around his head and his eyes looked like black marbles in the dark, wide and staring. He didn't know what Slocum would do, but he was gambling that Slocum wouldn't shoot and force him to blow out Charity's brains.

Ideas streaked through Slocum's mind. He was being asked to drop his gun, which meant giving up his life for Charity. Because Jessie, curse his black heart, wouldn't in a million years let him live. Not after the damage he'd done the Daltons.

One thought came with fierce clarity. He could chance a shot, because Charity's slender body did not give complete cover to Jessie's big bulk. But if his bullet did not stop Jessie dead, Jessie could still kill the girl. Jessie had the winning cards; Slocum couldn't let the girl die.

Somehow, with devilish luck, Jessie had survived in Sweetwater. The sound of two bullets fired before he pulled his gun had blunted his aim. What could he do now? Bow to the winning hand, that's what. And hope.

"Does she die, Slocum? What's it to be? Drop the gun."

Slocum dropped it. "You got it, Jessie." He put up his hands to give Jessie a sense of power, hoping he wouldn't shoot right off.

Jessie studied him, grinned broadly, then came forward, his Colt ready to fire. Slocum could see Charity's gun stuck in his belt. Jessie scooped up Slocum's gun and flung it into the bushes. He inhaled deeply, and his eyes glittered in the bright moonlight.

"For just a moment there, Slocum, I thought you were going to let the little lady go out." He grinned. "But I figured you right. You got a heart of gold. You wouldn't let the filly die. Even though she's the she-devil who brought Tad Dalton to grief." He glared at Charity, whose face was distorted with hate.

"Why didn't you shoot him, Slocum?" She demanded. "Why? Got water in your veins?"

Jessie laughed, showing big white teeth. "Whyn't you answer her, Slocum? Let's hear it. Why didn't you?"

"Just couldn't do it, Charity. He had us over a barrel."

Jessie glared. "You bet I did. I been on your tail right along, and you made a big mistake sleeping so far from this sweet piece." He looked at her. "I'd never treat her like that, not me."

Because Jessie kept talking, Slocum's nerves began to ease up. If he was not in a hurry to kill, it meant he had things on his mind. It would be smart to keep him talking, "I thought you were dead, Jessie." Slocum spoke conversationally, lowering his hands slowly.

"You don't kill Jessie Dalton that easy," he sneered, and put his hand to his head."You missed your shot. Just touched my temple, but it knocked me flat. Didn't take long to collect myself and pick up your trail." He grinned. "Sure made it easy when you teamed up with this honey." His eyes went over her figure and he licked his lips. "I thought Tad was a damned fool going for you, but now that I see you this close up, I can understand."

He strolled to a half-buried rock, sat down, lit a cheroot, and studied Slocum and Charity through slitted eyes. For a few minutes he just puffed the cheroot; then his jaw hardened.

"I ain't got much time. I aim to join Red, but first I gotta pay you off, Slocum, for all you done to the Daltons. Their bones are rottin' because of you. You're gonna die, but not easy."

He puffed some smoke and a vicious glint came to his yellow-brown eyes. "I'm gonna tell you what I aim to do, so you can think about it while you watch this pretty filly make love to me." He grinned. "Surprised? Yeah, I figure I owe it to Tad. He wanted her in the worst way and he paid a heavy price for it. We'll take care of O'Rourke. But first I'm goin' make him wish he hadn't done what he did to poor Tad." He smoked thoughtfully. "See that oak, Slocum? I'm goin' rope you naked to it, and in the heat of the day the buzzards are goin' to pick at your eyes and your balls, have a regular feast. Just keep thinkin' about that."

He turned suddenly to Charity, who'd been listening to him, her face twisted with horror.

It amused him. "What do you think of that?" he asked mockingly.

"You're not human, that's what I think of it," she said slowly.

Jessie gaped at her, then got up, walked to her, and slapped her hard. She stumbled back and fell. Slocum started and Jessie swung his gun. "Go ahead, but I won't kill you, just pick pieces off you." His voice was grim. "Gotta keep you alive for the buzzards."

He bent to Charity, who lay stunned. "Now you be a nice girl and I won't have to hit you again. You're too nice a filly to hit. What you need is lovin' not hittin'." He ripped at the buttons of her shirt, then pulled at her jeans, all the time watching Slocum. He soon had her naked, her white body gleaming in the light of the moon.

To Slocum she looked like Diana, the statue, shapely, beautiful, and this hyena was just about to ruin her. Although Slocum seemed to be a beaten man, standing slumped, his muscles were mobilized and he waited for a crucial moment. But Jessie, a wily dog, kept watching Slocum, kept his gun pointed, and a wrong move would send the bullets flying. Slocum, looking into the gun barrel, could easily see everything coming to an end on this godforsaken piece of ground. He watched Jessie through slitted eyes, praying for just one moment, just one.

Charity's naked body couldn't help but put a spell

on Jessie. His lips twisted, his eyes glittered. "Yeah, little girl, I never expected you to look this good." He rubbed his chin thoughtfully. "Now, as I tol' you, I'm in a hurry. No time to get my duds off. We'll just do a couple of things, enjoy ourselves while Slocum here watches. It's his last night, so let's give him a good show."

He calmly unbuttoned himself and his flesh came out sturdy with excitement. "Now you just come here and fondle this a bit. I guess you know how to do that; ol' Slocum here taught you. So do it, heah?" His voice rasped suddenly. "Because if you don't, I'm goin' put a bullet in yore pretty little ass."

Charity looked at Jessie with fear and loathing. She turned to Slocum and the look in her eyes wrenched his gut, but he stood there, the picture of defeat. He stared at her, hoping she'd read a message in his face. She tore her gaze from him, turned to run, but Jessie fired two shots that kicked up dirt in front of her.

She turned slowly. He grinned. "Come on, little sugar, you're goin' to love this thing. It's your lucky night. Come here."

She stood frozen.

He cocked his gun.

Her face set hard and, glancing again at Slocum, she walked past him toward Jessie. "Come closer," he purred. "You're goin' love this. Just give it a nice wet kiss."

She looked unsteady, leaned toward him, put out her hand, and Jessie, frantic with lust, watched, his eyes fastened on her every move. Suddenly, as if overwhelmed by disgust, she pushed him, struggled to grab his pistol hand. It was so unexpected that it put him off balance for a moment. But that was all

Slocum needed. Lightning-fast, he slid down to his boot and with one smooth motion pulled the throwing blade from its holster and flung it at Jessie's chest.

It slipped in up to the hilt.

Jessie's eyes shot open in shock, seemed to come out of their sockets; his gun fired wild and he stumbled back, fell, tried to pull the knife from his chest, then, with staring eyes, he struggled to bring the gun up to shoot Slocum. His arm, an inch at a time, came off the ground. Slocum watched calmly. Charity watched, frozen with terror.

Then his hand dropped, the gun fired, and Jessie fell back, staring with dead eyes at the sky.

9

Charity had watched Jessie in terror until he died. Then she turned to Slocum. Her light blue eyes glowed with a strange fire and she rushed to him and hugged him fiercely.

"Slocum, I thought you were a goner. Even with that knife stickin' in him, I thought he'd get you." She gazed up at his face. "I did you wrong. I figured you'd lost your nerve because you wouldn't shoot. You're a real man, Slocum. I'm sorry I cussed you out." And she put her head against his chest.

A shock went through Slocum as he felt her naked body. He could feel her breasts, her silky flesh. Some deep carnal urge rushed up from the pit of his being and, though he got his clothes off, he scarcely knew how. Killing Jessie seemed to have unleashed in him some primitive force, and the prize was woman. And here she was, female, beautiful and nude.

And Charity, her eyes big with amazement, was staring at him, down at his swollen lust. She couldn't make up her mind if he'd gone loco, yet she couldn't help feeling excitement at the sight of his inflamed desire.

He grabbed her, kissed her lips, his hands moving over her breasts, her belly, her buttocks, and then down between her thighs. He pressed her and she could feel his hardness against her flesh. She felt a powerful gush of sensation, both fear and desire.

Slocum, in the grip of frenzy, pushed her body to the ground, almost forced her thighs apart, and thrust into her, feeling her tight, warm, velvet wetness. She whimpered because he was big, because of his over-whelming force. He plunged deeply into her, holding tight to her buttocks. Even as he thrust, again and again, Slocum dimly felt he'd been grabbed by a mys-terious natural force. His hard, dynamic, staccato thrusts made her whine, but she felt powerless, hyp-notized.

After what seemed an eternity to her, she felt his great swelling, the surge of his climax, and he held her in a tight, almost suffocating embrace. To her amazement, she felt an extraordinary spasm of plea-sure in the depths of her body.

He stayed on her for a while, as if exhausted by his onslaught.

Then slowly he raised his body, looked down at her, and his green eyes, which had been strange and wild in his frenzy, now seemed calm, the way she remembered him.

But her mouth hardened; she knew she'd been violated.

The light of dawn was rosy as Slocum threw the last shovel of dirt on Jessie's grave. He leaned on the shovel and wiped his brow with his neckerchief. It had been hard to get Jessie dead, but there was no doubt he lay under this pile of dirt. He shot a glance at Charity, sipping coffee from her tin cup. Since his wild onslaught last night, she hadn't said two words to him.

Why did he go hogwild like that? It couldn't be Charity. She was a honey of a girl, but he'd had fine women before. It had to be something else. It had to do, he figured, with his fight, his death battle with Jessie. Jessie had the whip hand, was going to feed him to the buzzards. That idea, in spite of Slocum's cool front, had unleashed a lot of fear; it was a hell of a way to go. And when, at the last moment, he destroyed Jessie, all that fear raced through his body. It had to get out and Charity, throwing her beautiful naked body against his, was the lighted fuse that made him explode. He had screwed like a wild animal released from the threat of death. Charity's warm, vibrant body was life.

Slocum smiled. He felt he had the explanation. After the battle comes sex. It was like this with the stag and lion—why not man? When he packed the cups in the saddlebag, Charity's eyes were cold as ice. He smiled grimly, swung over the saddle, and she followed him on the gelding.

As the horses jogged along, his eyes scanned the terrain, and he suddenly shrugged. To hell with it; he couldn't worry about it. She should have been home like a good little girl instead of riding a territory that crawled with violence. He'd told her to get back to her father, but she wouldn't listen. She wanted to play with the big boys; she wanted to hunt down Red Dalton, a girl like her. It was a laugh.

Red's tracks led to the Santa Maria trail, which twisted toward the great western territories. Settlers used this trail, buffalo roamed it, Comanches raided it to protect their food supply. A single rider like Dalton could slip through unmolested, even two riders might, though, Slocum understood, the wild Comanche braves had a taste for young paleface squaws.

Slocum, who rode near the trees for cover, couldn't help grinding his teeth in frustration. He had to protect her against Comanches and desperados, but who protected her against him? She looked sullen and far away, and he didn't care for that. It seemed a part of her had enjoyed their encounter. But you didn't grab her like that, a young woman who not long ago had been a virgin. What the hell, he was no plaster saint. Why, at a time like that, had she thrown her naked body against him?

He loosened his neckerchief to wipe his brow. The sun hung like a yellow blaze in a cloudless sky. A bald eagle in majestic slow motion swung its mighty wings as it flew toward the mountain. The peaks thrust up great jagged sculptures of stone in the clear purity of the air.

He glimpsed a thin thread of smoke at least a mile off on the Santa Maria trail, and his heart sank. Smoke like that might be a Comanche attack, the start of a wagon burning. What would it be? A few wagons catching hell from Comanches? But with good rifles and smart thinking, the settlers could fight the Comanches off. If not, it would be a massacre, and even the thought made his jaw tighten.

"What is it, Slocum?" She had seen something in his face, not the rising smoke.

"It's a hot day," he said. No point in making her anxious about Comanches when he didn't know the facts.

"It's something else," she said, her face hard set. "But there's no use asking you."

He grimaced; she was a saucy, clever little honey, and she could read his face like a book.

"If there's no use asking, then let's just keep riding."

The roan's body gleamed with sweat in the pitiless heat. Slocum swung off the saddle and from his canteen poured water into his hat. The roan drank it, his big brown eyes looking gratefully at his rider. Charity gave water to her gelding.

"Could we stop for a few minutes, please?" The words were polite, and he wondered if the heat was melting her anger.

They moved under the leafy shade of a cottonwood and he brought out some hard biscuits. Though they were stale, she munched at the food without complaint. She did little complaining, he had to admit. Not about the food, the heat, or the hard riding. But she'd been cool and moody since last night, and it tired him. He was tired of thinking about her; it could get them both killed. In this land you didn't lose your concentration. An ambush could kill you in a moment. Dalton was out there, Comanches, O'Rourke's men, and who knew what else.

She cleared her throat. "How far ahead of us is Dalton, do you figure?" The blue eyes were cold in her pretty face.

"About six hours." He paused. "If we give up sleep time, we could close in faster."

"Whatever you decide," she said.

That was more like it. Could he expect her to drop her moody fit and be friendly again?

Her full lips pressed together and her brows came down. "You raped me last night, Slocum, didn't you?"

That jolted him. She knew how to hit a man in the gut. She had no humor in her face or tone.

"Just a friendly get-together." He smiled.

"Friendly! You were a hellcat on a rampage."

"Maybe I got carried away."

"Maybe! You got a funny way of using words, Slocum. I'm disappointed."

"That's how it goes," he said.

"I thought you were a gentleman."

He gritted his teeth. "Never claimed to be one." He pulled a havana from his breast pocket, lit it with a lucifer. She watched.

"I reckon, Charity, that if you're ever in a bad lash-up like the one last night, you don't throw your naked body against a man. Men are not made of stone."

She looked jarred, as if the idea never occurred to her. Then she scowled. "So it's my fault that you grabbed me and acted like a wild pig."

He had to smile; he had managed to blame her.

Her face was hard. "Never expected it from you. You were so gentle, so considerate the first night. I trusted you."

"There's a lesson there. Don't trust men. A beautiful young girl who happens to be naked is dynamite to all men. Keep it in mind."

Her blue eyes glittered like anthracite, drilling into him. "You're just an ornery ol' goat. And you're going to need me when that posse catches up."

He grinned. She was a spirited little thing and he had to try and stay a yard off her. "They ain't going to catch up unless you rope and throw me like a steer. Now let's move."

They rode for a time and the smoke on the trail, which had been a thin swirl, now looked thicker and darker.

It had to be a burning wagon, and Slocum couldn't help feeling sorry for the settlers who probably had caught hell from rampaging Comanches. Most settlers, even with rifles, were too inexperienced with Comanches, and no match for their cunning. The Comanche warrior was powerful and brave, and this was his land. Slocum in his time had seen their deadly work. They showed no mercy to the palefaces greedy to grab their land and destroy the buffalo, their source of life.

Slocum's piercing green eyes swept the trees, the boulders, the brush, and the trail, and it didn't take long for him to spot the two men coming toward them. One rode a spirited black horse, the other walked, pulling his horse, which looked lame. They wore wide-brimmed sombreros, chaps, and black shirts. As they came near, the rider on the black raised his hand in a friendly wave and smiled.

Slocum waved back. Clearly they were in trouble. A horse with a lame leg, and coming from the direction of a Comanche attack; but they were obviously not settlers. They were scruffy, and he didn't care for the look of them. "Stay out of it," he muttered to Charity. She frowned and her mouth tightened. As they came closer, he pulled up and swung off the roan. The other rider did the same, and both men, standing together, stared at Charity, amazed to discover she was a young woman.

"Howdy. Scotty is the name," said the rider, and he grinned, showing long yellow teeth. Under his sombrero was a foxy face, a sharp chin, small glittering black eyes that darted from the horses to Charity, as if he didn't believe she was a woman. "This is Burt." He jerked his thumb at the other, a stubble-bearded man with washed-out blue eyes, a sullen, turned-down mouth, and a dirty neckerchief at his throat. "Burt here has hard luck with his hoss, as you see," Scotty said with a devilish grin. He jerked his thumb behind him. "Comanches are having a fire party. We were headed that way, but figured it'd be smart to backtrack. We were runnin' hard, then this dumb hoss of his goes lame. Bad luck, eh, pardner?"

"Yeah, bad luck," Slocum said without smiling. "What about the settlers?"

Scotty stared at him. "What about them?"

Were they stupid, Slocum asked himself, or something much worse? "A couple of guns might have helped them," he said.

Scotty considered it, then nodded. "Could be, pardner," he said cheerfully. "But no redskin's goin' to get our scalps if we kin help it, are they, Burt?" He laughed boisterously and Burt joined in. He looked fascinated by Charity and her gelding; he couldn't keep his eyes off them.

"Say, cowboy," Burt said, "this filly's got a nice hoss. Like to buy it from her."

It's trouble, Slocum thought. They probably didn't have a dollar between them. He smiled slowly. "You got a fine sense of humor, mister. And what does she ride?"

"She can ride behind you, pardner," Scotty cackled. "We bring you two closer together. You wouldn't mind that."

Slocum was sorry that he'd stopped. He thought they might be part of the wagon under attack by the Comanches, but they were just a couple of trail bums, out to scavenge where they could. He had a situation here because they were after the gelding, and probably Charity, too. He had to set for it.

"I'll tell you, Scotty, we've got a long trip ahead, and we got to make time. We need both horses. I'm sorry about your trouble. You might double up on your horse and make it back to Sweetwater."

The small, mean eyes glittered and the thin lips widened. "The way I see it, pardner," said Scotty, "those Injuns might be coming this way, and we don't intend to be hobblin' till then. So it'd be a good idea to give us your hosses." He grinned. "You see, we aim to take *your* hoss, too. Just so you understand, we take the filly *and* we take your hosses." He stroked his chin, watching Slocum carefully. "Now you might think that greedy, but we'll let you live. And that's something. Right, Burt?"

"Yeah," said Burt, grinning gleefully at the idea. "He can go on breathing, but we take the hosses and the gal."

They grinned, standing side by side, enjoying the

joke. Charity looked pale, her lips tight as she watched Slocum.

Slocum grimaced. "You're a couple of jokers. You gave us some laughs. Now why don't you be good fellows and keep hobbling down the trail. You'll probably make it back to Sweetwater okay."

For a moment Scotty looked nervous; he didn't believe Slocum would have the nerve to face them. Then he put it down to play-acting in front of the girl.

"Pardner," he said slowly, his eyes slitted, "we got two guns to one. You can't come out of this in one piece. So be smart and step back from the hoss."

There was a sudden stillness, they all went for their guns. To Charity, Slocum's move was almost a blur. Two shots sounded like one. Scotty never got his gun out of the holster, for the bullet ripped his chest wide open, and Burt did get his gun just out of the holster, when the bullet tore through his neck, and the blood spurted in a jet. She shut her eyes.

Slocum studied the men, slipped his gun back into his holster, then glanced at Charity. She was white-faced, but managed a sickly smile. She swallowed. "Never saw shootin' like that, Slocum."

"Two less hyenas walking the earth," he growled as he dragged the men toward the bushes.

It took almost two hours before they reached the place in the trail where they'd seen the smoke. Though he could see no smoke now, the acrid smell of burned wood hit his nostrils.

"Is it wise," Charity asked, "to ride into this? Why ride into trouble?"

"There's no avoiding trouble on this trail," he said. "Dalton went through here, and where he goes, we go." He glanced at her pale, serious face. "Redskins don't stick around after an attack. They kill, burn, take, and run." He smiled. "I don't aim to ride in blind, Charity."

The trail went into a steep curving decline, and he climbed a rock and looked down at the twisting path with bushes and boulders on either side, then a sharp right turn. Perfect for ambush, Slocum thought. He studied every brush for the slightest quiver of bird, animal, or man.

He came down. "I'll ride ahead, you stay behind. Keep your gun handy," he told the girl.

His own gun out, he rode to where the trail twisted, sharply dismounted, and signalled to her to stop. He crawled forward, then saw the wagons, two of them, one already a blackened, burned hulk. He could smell whiskey, saw the broken empty bottles against the wheels. Two men were lying face down, scalped, with arrows in their bodies. Two women in their thirties lay sprawled on their backs, one naked, a slash on her throat, the other with her dress hiked up, her thighs spread and bloody. Two young boys lay face up, strangled.

Slocum studied the moccasin prints. Three Comanches had ambushed the drivers with arrows from behind the bushes. The settlers never had time to use their rifles. The Comanches strangled the screaming-kids, jumped the women, strangled one. It was war without quarter; these Comanches were merciless and revengeful. They hated the palefaces who were stealing their land. They were in war to the death. Their tracks went west, then into the brush and up the slope. It had all happened, he guessed from the fresh prints, about two hours before.

Charity rode up, pulling the roan. Her face paled as she gazed at the ruin. After a while, she asked, "How many Comanches?"

"Only three," he said grimly, thinking that if Scotty and his partner had been the right sort of men, this might have been avoided.

He pulled his shovel. There was a posse racing toward him and Dalton racing away, but he couldn't leave these unfortunate folk to the coyotes.

The sun was still overhead when he got the last body in the mass grave. His jaw was clenched. The redskins couldn't be too far. They were a menace not only to small settler wagons but to his own moves. He had Charity with him, and she'd be a red flag to a Comanche brave. He had to face them, and the sooner the better. The Comanches had been guzzling and when they drank too much it numbed their instincts. If he was going to hit them, the best time would be now.

He studied the prints. They'd gone up the steep slope which jutted against the rocks. Up there he might find a crevice, a cover where they might still be guzzling.

He turned to Charity. She'd helped him to drag the bodies to the grave, though her teeth were clenched. She was a brave girl.

"I'm going up there. I'll be back," he said.

She just stared; she knew what he had in mind.

"There's no way past them," he said. "They'll pick us up later. It'd be better for me to try to hit them now while they're muddled by whiskey. Later the odds will be with them."

Her blue eyes gleamed. "Perhaps if we waited for the posse."

He shook his head. "It'd be all over by then. And your father is as bad as the Comanches for my money."

"I'll go with you," she said. Her face was pale, but her lips were tight with resolution.

He laughed. "You're a great girl, Charity, but the Comanches would smell you a mile away. Just hang on here, near that tree. Keep your gun handy. Stay low. If I'm not back by mid-afternoon, you'd better ride toward Sweetwater. You'll probably run into your father and his friends."

10

He stared up the slope; it had brush, twisted trees, and boulders, and near the top bulked against a craggy mount. The prints went straight up, and unless he was reading it wrong, up there three Comanches were still drinking or sleeping off the whiskey. The problem: where were they? The way to find out was to get there. And do it like a Comanche, silently, invisibly. He started slowly, crawling through grass, behind brush and boulder, taking care never to move until everything was right. When a blackbird settled on a tree branch nearby, he stayed motionless until the bird flew off on its own whim. A startled bird, as he knew, as Comanches knew, flew differently. He crawled up and thought of why the Indian always took the high ground; it was best for attack and defense.

As he inched his way up, the heat beat down, so

that when he reached thirty feet from the top, his body was drenched in sweat. He could feel the beat of his heart, but his nerves were steady; he was trying to nail three Comanches, a decision made only because he reckoned they'd be whiskey-sodden. A fair-sized boulder bulked to his left only ten feet from the top. He would crawl there to work out his strategy. His knife was in his hand and his gun in his belt for quick use. He stopped and strained to hear. Not a sound. Nothing. Baffling. Drunken Indians were rarely silent. Could he be wrong about their position? But the prints were unmistakable. They were here somewhere. It took a long, slow time of crawling to reach the boulder, and its iron-grey massiveness gave him a sense of comfort. It was big, broad, gored by time and weather. He was relieved to be there; nothing was riskier than to be out in the open. During his crawl he'd half expected to hear the whoosh of an arrow. Long ago he had acquired a healthy respect for Comanche cunning. He thought of Charity, alone down below, and it put the edge on him. He didn't have much time. He'd have to close in faster.

It was then that he heard the whisper of a sound, the almost silent kind of sound only an Indian could make. His nerves screamed and he wheeled. The Comanche was there, his black eyes glaring, red paint fierce on his broad face. He came in a rush, knife in his hand, raised to strike. Slocum never stopped to think. His moves were all intuitive. His powerful arm went up to catch the Comanche at the wrist, and with the knife in his other hand he slashed at the Comanche's throat. There was a gurgle and a strangling sound, then the gush of blood as the Comanche fell, collapsing like an empty bag.

There hadn't been much sound, but whatever it

was, Slocum felt it more than enough for the other two. He'd completely misjudged their whereabouts, believing them on top and too drunk to expect attack. Instead, they'd seen him coming and set the ambush for *him*.

Now Slocum's mind raced furiously. What of the other two? Where were they? In the rock pile? Or had they with Indian cunning been watching the moves he had made with Charity? Alarm streaked through him, and he crossed the boulder and, crouching, started down, when the earth seemed to rise in front of him, and there they were, the two of them, separated by fifteen feet, their eyes glaring, their red faces in a fury, the one on the right with his tomahawk raised to crush Slocum's skull. Sliding left, away from them, Slocum pulled his gun with blinding speed, firing instantly at the head of the Comanche whose arm, holding the tomahawk over Slocum, went nerveless as the Indian seemed to melt toward the ground. The other Comanche struck at Slocum's gun hand with his tomahawk and only the quick twist of Slocum's arm saved it from breaking like a cornstalk. Still, the hurt to the muscle made it suddenly numb, and his gun dropped. The Comanche pushed his advantage, swung the tomahawk again, but he was too close, and Slocum grabbed his wrist with his good hand and twisted, bearing down with his body, putting every inch of his strength into the twisting. He felt the bones of the wrist snap as the Indian grunted.

The Comanche sprang back and reached with his left hand for the knife in his belt. He was not big, but he was sinewy. He had a broad face, gleaming black eyes, and long, coal-black hair. He smelled of whiskey.

Slocum moved back, aware that the numbness in

his right arm was fading. He had only his left arm but so did the Comanche. The black eyes glittered with hate as he started toward Slocum. He crouched, wary of Slocum's strength, hoping for an opening. He ripped at Slocum, who jumped back, stumbled, and, because he was on the downside of the slope, began to roll. The Comanche, frantic at this chance, raced after Slocum, stooped to plunge the knife, but Slocum jerked his leg violently, toppling him on his back. Slocum jumped on him, feeling strength returning to his right arm. He forced the Comanche's knife hand to the ground, held it, staring into the black, glowing eyes as the redskin strained to get free. The smell of his muscled body was strong in Slocum's nostrils. He slowly brought his right hand over, forcing the sturdy wrist back and back. He kept the squirming, wiry body under him, forcing and forcing until the stubby, sweaty hand opened and the knife fell to the earth. In a flash, Slocum had it and plunged it into the muscled chest all the way. The Comanche shuddered, went still, groaned a little, and his eyes looked at Slocum as his body seemed to wilt. Then the eyes just stared sightlessly.

Slocum struggled to his feet. Every bone in his body ached. The wound in his shoulder had reopened during the scuffling and had started to bleed. He still felt a touch of numbness in his left arm. His muscles had gone through rack and ruin, but there were three dead Comanches.

He had cleared the trail, and for one reason: Red Dalton.

Somewhere ahead his quarry lurked and there could be no rest until he caught up with Dalton.

He came down the slope cautiously, because long

ago he'd learned to move with care even when the land looked safe. The flicker behind a bush brought out his gun in a flash. Then he heard her.

"It's me, Slocum." He scowled; it had been a dumb trick for her to be on this slope. Only an intuitive feeling had stopped him from shooting first and asking later.

When she came out, gun in hand, he stared at her. "What the hell are you doing here? I told you to stay at the oak."

"You were a long time, and I heard the gun. Figured you might need help," she said cheerfully.

"Almost got yourself shot," he growled. Her eyes surveyed his clothes and body.

"They rough'd you up plenty," she said, concern in her voice. He shrugged. "They were tough. Lucky they'd been drinking."

When they came down, he asked, "Where are the horses?"

"I put them back in the cottonwoods just in case someone might be passing through."

He nodded. "That's the idea. Now let's move. We've got a lot of travelling."

In an effort to cut lost time, he rode hard, and she kept up. The gelding's stamina surprised him. It was strong-hearted, with a lot of lung power and speed. And plenty of spirit, like its mistress.

He smiled at her gutsiness, coming up the slope to help him with the Comanches. Gutsy; but she couldn't be too bright.

The land became lush as they rode, the grass greener, and yellow and purple wildflowers spotted the earth. The sun started its downward slide and lost its heat. Dalton's tracks stayed on the trail headed to

Dawson. A light, dry breeze sprang out of the west. It felt cool against his cheek. The roan's ears were up. *Smells water*, Slocum thought, and it didn't take long for them to reach a slow-flowing stream. The horses moved into it to drink. Slocum pulled off his clothes and splashed around. She stared at him, then turned her back.

"Are you going to wash up or stay sweaty?" he called.

She didn't answer, just walked downstream, where she went behind a bush.

The clean, cool water did a lot of good for his bruises, and he came out invigorated. After dressing, he glanced downsteam and, to his surprise, saw Charity floating. The sight of her white body with its sensual curves hit him with a shock. He turned away. She was a temptation, and she did devilish things to his body. He wished to hell she didn't put herself on display; it was more than the flesh of man could stand. But he'd be strong; from now on she was untouchable. He'd been rough with her and couldn't again yield to such impulses.

He tried not to look at her, but at the same time he wished she wouldn't expose herself. But she did have to bathe, didn't she?

When they started to ride again, he glanced over. She looked fresh as a spring flower. Her eyes gleamed blue as the Texas sky, and her white skin glowed with health. She was a honey if ever he saw one.

She caught his glance. "And what are you staring at, mister?"

"One beautiful girl," he said.

Her brows came down. "Just keep your mind on

what we're here for: *Red Dalton*."

He scowled. "If you weren't here to muddle my head, I could do that much better."

Her chin lifted. "I told you, I've got more of a grievance than you to see that Red Dalton gets his just deserts."

He shrugged and they rode in silence while the sun moved halfway down the sky.

Then he stiffened and held up his hand. They pulled to a stop. "There's something up ahead," he said. "You stand by while I look into it." He looked at her sharply. "You do as I say."

She nodded, reined her horse, and moved toward the brush. He walked the roan forward and spotted two men on the trail, one lying face down, the other kneeling, looking upset. Two horses stood to the side. Slocum stared hard at the men. The one kneeling was clean-looking, husky, with a brown shirt, shoelace tie, and chaps. He looked at Slocum a long moment, then held up his hand, a friendly greeting.

Slocum moved forward, studying the situation. The man on the earth looked knocked out, though there was no mark on him. Slocum had heard no shooting.

As Slocum swung off the roan, the kneeling cowboy stood up. He was dark-eyed, square-faced, sinewy, alert. "His horse got spooked by a rattler and threw him. Hit his head. He's out."

Slocum glanced at the earth and, sure enough, there was a dead rattler lying there, killed with a branch.

"Is he hurt bad?"

"Looks it," the cowboy said, and rubbed his chin, brooding. "Caine's the name," the cowboy said.

"Slocum."

"Maybe you could give me a hand lifting him to his hoss. I'll ride him into Dawson. Maybe they got a doctor there."

Slocum nodded and bent to the cowboy lying on his belly, helped turn him carefully, and found himself looking into a pistol. The cowboy's eyes were open and he was grinning.

"Well, Slocum," said Caine, also grinning broadly, "we picked you off easy as a dumb turkey. I'll take your gun."

Slocum glared at him.

"The gun," said Caine, "or we'll plug you now. We don't have to deliver you to O'Rourke." He grinned again. "He said to shoot your balls off if you troubled us. That's his orders."

Slocum's jaw tightened as he handed the gun to Caine, who stuck it in his belt. He looked at the cowboy lying down.

"Okay, Lowshot Joe, you did your job. You gonna stay there like a sleepin' beauty all night?"

Lowshot Joe got up and brushed his pants. "The best little actor this side of Texas," he said boastfully, and stared at Slocum. "So this is the dirty skunk who raped our little Charity? Why don't we just shoot him fulla holes now, Caine? Save the boss a lot of trouble."

Caine glowered. "Sometimes, Lowshot, I think you got the brains of a chicken." He turned to Slocum. "Where's Charity? And you better come clean, mister, 'cause we ain't in the mood to play games. We been riding a long time for this moment, and we don't have much patience left."

Slocum looked at him. He was not a big man, but he looked fast as a ferret. Lowshot Joe was rosy-cheeked with fair skin, wiry, compact, with mild grey eyes.

"Can I ask a question, Caine? How in hell did you get in front of me?"

Caine smiled. "We been riding like hell to do that, Slocum. We had the best horses in the posse, so they sent us ahead. We did with little sleep, and when you stopped to play with the Comanches it gave us enough time to set up this little trap." His face grew hard. "Now that we satisfied your curiosity, you'd better satisfy ours. Where's the girl?"

Slocum jerked a thumb. "Back there, waiting."

Caine's face looked grim. "You hurt her, mister, you're buzzard meat tonight."

Slocum spoke slowly. "She's okay."

"Start walking," Caine ordered, his gun pointing.

They walked back, and when Charity saw them she scowled and came out of the brush. "Is that you, Caine?"

He grinned. "It's us, Miss Charity. We got this ornery polecat. Your dad's about four hours back. He'll be coming up with Barry and Steele." He scowled. "Tell us right off. Did this lowdown critter harm you in any way? Your dad told us what to do if he did." His face was grim and threatening.

She gazed at them, then looked at Slocum. A mischievous glint in her eyes gave Slocum one hell of a moment. Then she said, "No, he didn't do anything. He behaved himself real good."

Caine looked a bit disappointed. He seemed to have been fascinated by the idea of shooting a man's balls off, Slocum thought.

"Well," Caine said grudgingly. "I'm shore glad

you ain't the worse for wear." He pulled out a cigarillo and lit it. "What in tarnation made you hightail outa the ranch quicker'n a wink? Yore dad is fittin' to be tied 'bout that, Miss Charity." He puffed his cigarillo. "Now my orders is if we catch you to take you into Dawson, where yore daddy will catch up with us." He moved easily near her, and quick as a flash he had her gun out of its holster.

She glared at him. "Are you crazy, Caine? Give me that gun."

"Cain't do it, Miss Charity. I hated doing it, but them's my orders. It's your dad's orders, and he must know why he's doin' it."

"Caine, you'll be sorry for this."

He looked miserable. "Only obeying orders, Miss Charity." He turned to Lowshot, who was smiling amiably. "Don't just set there. Tie this polecat's hands so we don't get any trouble while we're ridin'. He looks slick as a weasel to me."

Lowshot Joe shrugged and got a rope from his saddle. While Caine held the gun, Slocum's wrists were tied in front of him, which made him grieve. Caine, he thought, though he looked dumb, was a crafty dog. He done a couple of shrewd things. That trap on the road, grabbing Charity's gun, and tying Slocum's hands. He talked like a thickhead, but every move so far was smart.

Now what?

Charity was still free-handed, and if she could be shrewd, she might help. When he looked at her, however, she gave him just a blank face. Was she going to let them take him in and not lift a finger? She seemed content with the way things were going, seemed to like the idea of two cowboys from her father's ranch giving her escort. Maybe she had been more scared than he thought by the violence on the trail, particularly his brand. Probably she felt safer with them. He bit his lip. After all, he had grabbed her. She couldn't care for that, but he thought she had softened up and understood.

Well, he'd been mistaken. She kept a grudge. He wondered if she realized what it would mean if O'Rourke got hold of him. "Let's turn this stallion into a canary," he'd said, and the words were burned in Slocum's mind.

After a couple of hours they came to a small stream and stopped to let the horses drink. The cowboys brought out beef jerky and beans and biscuits.

"Aren't you goin' to untie my hands for eating?" Slocum demanded.

Caine smiled. "Listen to this geezer. You oughta be glad we're letting you eat. If we put a bullet in you we'd all have more food."

Joe said, "It's because Charity told us you wiped out the Comanche raiders that we're being so good to you."

He glanced at Charity calmly eating. She looked at him with her cool cornflower-blue eyes, then turned to Caine. "Oh, I didn't tell you, did I? Slocum also took care of Jessie Dalton."

Caine's brows knitted, and he looked startled, then turned to Slocum, his eyes a bit more respectful. "So you took out Jessie, did you? Well, that musta been a man-sized job. Jessie was one poisonous critter." He bit into his beef jerky and added, "Good riddance. I knew Jessie, and there's only one rattler meaner than him, and that's Red Dalton."

He spoke to Charity. "Don't understand, Miss

Charity, why you'd want to run off and try and hunt down Red Dalton by yourself with this cowboy. He did you a bad mischief, and he's gotta pay. As for Red, we'll get him sooner or later. Your dad never gives up. And when we do, we're gonna lengthen his neck."

"If you get him," Slocum said. "He won't be sitting around."

"We'll get him," Caine said confidently.

Lowshot stared at Slocum with a critical eye, then shook his head. "It's a mystery to me, Miss Charity why you run out from your daddy's ranch after this polecat. You being a real young lady who, when you're growed up, could get the best cowboy in the county. Not a danged riding fool of a Texan would turn down the chance of a girl like you. It was a wild mornin' when you woke up to take after him."

Charity smiled at him coyly. "Would you have yourself in mind as one of the cowboys, Lowshot?"

He grinned ear-to-ear, his blue eyes gleaming with pleasure at the thought. "Why, shore, Miss Charity, you can put me down on the list."

Charity glowered at Slocum. "I figured this mean polecat was going after Red Dalton, and I wanted something fierce to be there and do some shooting into Dalton. Slocum ain't much, but he can sure hunt down a man. I told you, he did get Jessie. That gave me a lot of satisfaction, Lowshot."

Caine gazed at her. "You shore have the spirit of your dad, Miss Charity. I expect when we catch up with Dalton you'll put a lotta holes in him. And, as for this ornery polecat, we'll give you plenty of revenge on him. We've got some mean things in mind."

Charity looked at Slocum with a curled lip. "The

worst is too good for this one. I'm looking forward to that."

Caine and Lowshot Joe listened to her with pleasure and turned a hard look at Slocum.

"We better go on toward Dawson. No point hanging out here. Never know what they hit you with."

They broke camp, and Slocum noted again how she avoided his eye, and instead flirted with Lowshot, who appeared to be one of her favorites.

They rode another hour and the sun started to sink. Slocum because of his tied wrists, found the riding irksome, and his body ached from his fight with the Comanches. At no time did Charity look at him, and he felt bitter about her. He'd let himself be horn-swoggled into taking her along, though his instinct had argued loudly against it. Just as he'd expected, she became the albatross around his neck. He'd stopped on the trail because of her, not to wear her out, and keep the trail clear. If she'd not been dragging on him, he could have skirted most of the obstacles, kept a hard pace on Dalton, caught up with him by this time. She was the cause of his trouble, and now these scruffy cowhands had him tied like a deadhead turkey, lugging him into Dawson to meet that sinister gentleman, Sean O'Rourke.

He'd made mistakes of course, but it was always because of Charity that he had stopped. She seemed to have no sense of obligation. To have forgotten what Jessie was about to do to her, what Scotty and his mangy partner would have done. And the Comanches—God help her if she had fallen into their hands.

She was riding behind him. Her face was stony, and he glared at her, then turned. He sure had some wrong ideas about that girl.

Why did she turn on him? Probably she never did forgive him for the way he roughed her up after that fight with Jessie. It made her think differently about him. She was too young; didn't understand men. Fate sure kicked him in the teeth when it sent Charity into his life.

He shifted his bulk. He felt saddle-sore because his tied hands threw off his rhythm of riding.

They traveled another hour through rocky, hilly country, and Slocum's eyes narrowed as he scrutinized it. Caine was riding into it as if he had no care in the world. Not a trail-smart cowboy, Slocum thought. In such places Slocum always checked the land and stayed behind cover.

Caine turned to Charity. "Tired, Miss Charity?"

"Could do with a short break in the ridin' and a drink," she said.

They pulled up near a big boulder, swung off the horses, and took out the canteens. The two men and Charity stood, while Slocum dropped wearily against the boulder, his legs drawn up, his hands between them.

"Your dad said we'd all meet at the saloon in Dawson," said Caine. "We'll put you in the hotel while we scout for Dalton. He's got friends there. We hafta be mighty careful in Dawson."

Lowshot was looking at Charity, and it was clear he was smitten. "It's a mighty shame, Miss Charity, that you have to do all this ridin' because of this polecat here. The more I think about him, the more I feel inclined to do the job myself, without waitin', punish him for the dirty trick he did you."

She smiled seductively at him. "I think, Lowshot, you got a soft spot in your heart for Charity O'Rourke."

"You don't doubt that, do you?" he demanded. "Just you tell me, and I'll put my hand into fire for you."

She smiled brilliantly, sauntered up behind him, reached to kiss his cheek, then pulled his gun, stepped back and pointed it at Caine.

"Drop your guns, Caine." Her voice was hard.

He just stared. "Have you gone plumb loco, Miss Charity?"

She fired a shot at his feet.

He danced back and threw the guns. "All right, all right."

Slocum was sitting at the boulder watching her, amazed. She motioned Lowshot to move back.

Slocum stood up, standing next to the boulder. "Cut these ropes," he said, shoving his hands at her.

She gave him a look. "It might be safer to take you along tied up."

His mouth fell open. Then he saw the mischievous gleam in her eye. "It's not the way I want to meet Red Dalton," he said.

"No," she agreed with a small smile and, watching the two men standing together facing the boulder, she moved to Slocum, bent to his boot, pulled the knife, and ripped the cords. Quickly he picked up the gun on the ground, holstered it, and put the other in his belt.

Then the sound boomed off the rocks, and Lowshot went back as if he'd been hit by a mule, fell, his gut a bloody mass of red. Slocum, near the boulder, grabbed Charity and jerked her down to the earth. A second boom and the rifle bullet tore the skull off Caine's head. He was dead before he hit the ground.

Then the silence.

Lying flat against the boulder, Slocum felt safe. It had been the only reason he'd not been shot first; the boulder had screened him from the rifleman. Where was he shooting from? Had to be high on the ridge shaped like a saddle behind him. Whoever it was had a Sharps rifle and a commanding position. It had to be Dalton. He had stopped cleverly to wipe out his trackers.

"Stay down," he whispered to Charity. Her blue eyes were in shock as she looked at the ranch men sprawled in bloody death. She brought her hand to her mouth to stifle a cry.

He crawled flat to the other side of the boulder. Five feet away another big rock bulked safely. He would move, try to draw fire, smoke out the position of the gunman. He waited a moment, then dashed across the open space. He reached the boulder as the bullet splintered stone. There was no doubt that the fire came from a ledge on the ridge that looked squarely down on the trail.

Slocum could think of no way to get to him. His own rifle in the saddle holster was on his roan, and it grazed in the wooded area fifty feet away.

Then he heard Dalton's voice booming down. "Hey, Slocum, you're gonna die like a dog." He laughed. "Tell you what. Send the little bitch up here and I'll let you live a little while longer."

Quick as a wink, Slocum brought up his gun and fired at the sound. He did not expect to hit Dalton, but it might give him something to think about.

In a stupid rage, Dalton fired twice, hitting the boulder.

Now what? Slocum crouched behind the boulder and glanced up. The sun was creeping behind the mountain, and within the half-hour it would be too dim for good shooting. Charity had turned her face to the boulder, hard hit by the death of the ranch men. It was a safe position and, though Dalton was a hyena, he wouldn't shoot a woman. Slocum thought about Dalton. He was crafty. He wouldn't go into Dawson until he'd cleared the trail of whoever was tracking him. He didn't stop much on the way until he made it to here. It was a bristling saddle of a ridge and from it you had the sun behind you and a commanding view of all riders. He had probably waited a long time for his quarry to appear. Though Dalton wanted Slocum in the worst way, he had to settle for Caine and Lowshot, whom he probably recognized as O'Rourke's men.

Slocum figured Dalton had two choices: to wait in hope of getting a good shot or move to force the play. Slocum watched the sun slip behind the peaks and the light dim. In a short time nobody could shoot worth a damn. And then Slocum could get his own Sharps rifle, which reduced the odds.

It might be a good idea to throw a shot or two at Dalton's position, to let him know he couldn't move without risk. He used the side of the boulder to protect his head, peered out and fired, then jerked back. A bullet chipped the boulder. Well, Dalton had to realize he didn't have it all his own way.

The long shadows started, then the gloom of twilight. Nothing was happening up on the ledge. He glanced at Charity, huddled against the boulder, still turned away from the two dead cowhands. He might be lying there himself if he had not, with his sense of natural caution, taken a protective position behind the boulder.

There was nothing to do now but wait for dark.

11

After it had been dark for half an hour, Slocum crawled to Charity, took her hand, and pulled her fifty feet away, behind a big, bulking rock that gave good cover. A dim half-moon started up on the horizon. Then he crawled to the horses and got her bedroll and his Sharps rifle.

He whispered, "Get some shuteye. Later in the night I'll be going up there."

She gazed at him. "I don't like it."

He frowned. "Why?"

She looked away. "I don't know. Even if you could get up there, it's not good. He might be waiting. He could hear you. And if, in spite of everything, you managed to get him, it's not the way I want him dead." She leaned toward him, her voice intense. "I want to *see* him killed. I want to put some bullets in his disgusting body. To see him just dead up there would never be enough."

She had a hell of a lot of O'Rourke in her, he thought.

"I'd like to oblige you, Charity, but if we do nothing, in the morning he'll again have the upper ground, and we'll be pinned down."

She looked thoughtful. "Why not just ride to Dawson? He must be going there."

He rubbed his cheek. "We can't be completely sure. If he sees our tracks to Dawson, he could veer off, go anywhere. There's gold stashed somewhere, and that may be where he's heading."

"That'll be all the more reason to follow him."

He shook his head. "He's got the edge if he stays up there. He knows we want him bad, and that we'll stay." He stared at the half-moon beginning its climb. "Not too much light; it's a good night to bushwhack him."

"It's not how I see it," she said, and lay down on the bedroll. She was tired. It had been a long day, and two of her friends were lying dead out there.

"I'll think about it," he said. "Get some rest meanwhile."

He thought about it, and the more he thought, the more reason he found to go up there. Red Dalton was a killer without mercy, but the best reason of all was that at this moment he knew where Dalton was, and at any other time he could never be sure. A bird in the hand... Of course, it would be ticklish as hell, climbing that ridge to nail him. He could be sitting there, just waiting, convinced Slocum was the kind of man who'd make that climb. The trick, of course, was to come at him from a position he was not expecting.

He shut his eyes for a time, giving himself a wake-up signal in two hours, and the way he slept, he could hear the sounds of night. And nothing he heard alerted him.

When he opened his eyes the moon was almost overhead, and he glanced at Charity; she slept peacefully enough, her face almost translucent in the moonlight. A lovely girl, he thought as he silently picked up his gun. He decided not to take the Sharps after all; it would bog him down.

So far Red Dalton hadn't done anything dumb. In fact, he'd done the smart thing, and Slocum was hard set not to underestimate him.

He moved lightly and quietly to the west of the ridge, then started creeping up the side, silent as a ghost, listening to every night sound. As he moved, step by step, he tried never to offer an open shot, aware that, even in this dim moonlight, a bullet could hit him.

More than once, he wondered if he'd done the right thing, leaving Charity asleep, unaware of danger. But it would be a miracle if Dalton could get behind him, the way the ridge and the land were set up.

After laborious, silent movement that took more than an hour, he got to within thirty feet of where he'd seen Dalton raise his rifle, his hideout. Slocum stood silent and strained his ears for the sound of a man sleeping. He could hear his own breathing, feel his own heartbeat, but nothing else.

He stood like a statue, uncertain of his next move. He could hear a coyote wail, and the scraping of a small animal who hunted at night. Suddenly he stiffened. It was a solid body moving through the brush. His gun barked, and immediately he heard the animal yelp, then the heavy fall.

That was it! He'd hit the wrong animal and jolted the hell out of Dalton, who by now must have grabbed his rifle.

Slocum made a lightning decision, and dashed like a crazy horse into Dalton's hideaway, shooting wild on the idea that he'd be sleep-heavy and move sluggishly.

And that was what he did, sprinting forward, twisting from side to side just in case Dalton and his rifle suddenly rose up.

But he didn't, and Slocum rushed behind the bulky stone wall, shooting into it even before he could see, and when he could see, there was nothing. In the dim moonlight he could see only spent rifle shells on the ground, the prints of Dalton's boots; but he was gone. Been gone for hours, probably. The tracks went down the backside of the ridge to the flat land where he'd tied his horse. He had made his getaway. It was odd, because he did have the superior firing position.

But he had to know that, come dark, Slocum could get his Sharps rifle, which lessened the odds.

When he came back down off the ridge to her bedroll, he found her with her eyes open. She sat up.

"I heard the shots," she said, "and feared for you."

He smiled. "They were my shots. He wasn't there."

She stared. "He's gone?"

He nodded. "Crept away in the night like a skunk. And I spent an hour trying to get up there real quiet. Shot a coyote instead."

She was gazing at him almost tenderly. "I'm glad you're back in one piece, Slocum."

Her voice, so warm, almost caressing, touched him. She needed cuddling bad, he felt, especially after this brutal day. As he came near, she put out her hand and pulled him close. He bent and kissed her; her lips were soft. He felt her breath come fast and put his arms tight about her. He felt her breasts against his chest, and his hands stroked her body. The curve of her back, the sweep of her hips, the smooth skin of her neck, the roundness of her buttocks. He felt the prod of desire but, remembering their last encounter, he hesitated to move boldly.

They were pressed to each other, and she must have felt his swollen excitement, for her hand moved down to caress him. That did it for him.

She was a sexy young woman in misery at the moment, who needed a lot of loving, whose body craved fulfillment.

He unbuttoned her shirt, and she leaned back to make it easy. He reached down to her breast, its tip alert with excitement, cupped it in his hand, pleasuring in its smoothness, and put his tongue to the nipple, playing with it, which made her sigh deeply. He did this for a few moments, then she, with sudden boldness, reached down to unbutton his jeans.

His organ came out, rigid and swollen, and she gazed at it, amazed, then brushed her lips along the length, caressed it, then drew it into the vibrant warmth. It sent a jolt through him to see her beautiful face like that, especially when she adventured with her tongue. It was astonishing how swiftly she'd learned the arts of love. He tore off his clothes, as did she. Her white body seemed to glow in the moonlight. His hands couldn't get enough of caressing her pear-shaped breasts with their hard nipples, her silky, rounded buttocks. He looked at the pink-lipped crease between her thighs, shyly covered with blonde fringe, and reached into the wet smoothness. She lay in a trance as he stroked her over and over. Then he slipped past her rounded buttocks into her, held her breasts, and began to move. She was tight, and each movement made her sigh with pleasure. After a time, he turned her on her back and plunged into her. She inhaled sharply, as if she'd been hit with a club, and lay there, the curves of her body silky in the moonlight. He moved his hips, coming out, then in, and at each thrust a gasp escaped her. Again and again he thrust and her body picked up his rhythm, coming to meet him. Now he was gentle to the same degree that he'd been rough with her before, and she responded ecstatically.

Then her body suddenly wrenched, her teeth gritted, and she seemed to try to push her way through his bulk. Her body shook in the grip of a raging climax. Slocum went into his own frenzy, and began to plunge as hard as he could, over and over. He finally swelled mightily as he felt his searing surge.

She almost screamed through her clenched teeth.

They stayed together tightly for a long time, then slowly unwound.

The moon, Slocum became aware, had become a bright, glittering eye, as if it had been peeping on their lovemaking. His mind seemed to open to the sounds of night, the cry of the hawk, the baying of the coyotes.

If ever a woman needed a bit of loving, he was thinking, it was at a time like this. When the world looked dangerous, death near, and the future uncertain.

Charity had reached out for love. Maybe she expected Dalton to cut him down, and she wanted something from him. Maybe fear aroused her need for love. Women were strange, he thought, as he crawled to his bedroll.

There was, he reckoned, about three hours till dawn, and he sure could use the rest.

The next morning Slocum poked around until he found Dalton's tracks far behind the ridge.

"He's gone to Dawson," he said.

She nodded. She looked more herself this morning, fresh, perky, and ready to ride, ready for revenge. Her cornflower-blue eyes gazed at him softly, as if she remembered last night. Then her jaw hardened as she thought of Dalton.

"Let's get him," she said.

They swung over their horses and rode hard, stopping one time to let the horses drink, and two hours before sundown they reached Dawson.

Main Street looked lively with cowpunchers booted, spurred, and belted, and there were plenty of derelicts and desperadoes among the good citizens. To Slocum it looked as if a lot of seamy rascals in the territory had found their way to this town.

"Go to the hotel while I look in the saloon," he said.

Charity grimaced. "But I want to be there."

He scowled. "Leave it to me. I'll take care of it."

"I want to be there," she said doggedly. "I want

to see that polecat catch hell."

He stared at her, frustrated.

"Red Dalton," she said, "is smart as a rattlesnake. You'll need my help."

"You could get your pretty head shot off," he growled.

Her mouth tightened, but he stopped her. "Look, honey, you could do with a hot bath. Get yourself cleaned off. You got a peck of dirt on you, and it ain't womanly. And eat some steak, yams, and corn. A good dinner. I'll be there to join you soon."

She bit her lip. The idea of cleaning up did appeal to her, as well as the thought of a good hot meal. But she had done a lot to get here, come a long way, crossed her dad, gone through the dangers of the trail. If there was to be a showdown, she wanted to be in on it.

Slocum took off his Stetson and mopped his brow. "He may not be there," he said reasonably. "I'll come back for you if I hear he is."

"You promise?" Her eyes were intense.

"Promise," he said, thinking that in special cases, promises need not be kept. He watched her ride to the Dawson Hotel.

He walked his horse down the street, past Hawkins' Livery, Mama Joy's Café, Wilson's General Store, until, at the end of the street, he reached O'Toole's Saloon.

He tied the roan to the hitching rail and pushed through the batwing doors.

12

It was a crowded saloon, men drinking at the bar and playing cards at the tables, but no sign of Red Dalton. Dalton was a big, red-bearded hulk who'd stand out anywhere. At the bar, the drinkers were boisterous, and at the tables, the players were concentrating on their cards. Everyone was drinking. A sprinkling of women in yellow dresses snuggled close to men at the back tables.

When Slocum came in, hardly anyone looked at him, just a lean-faced gambler sitting at a card table, who seemed to be watching the doors. Slocum ordered whiskey from the bald-headed, mustached barkeeper wearing an apron. The barkeep scrutinized Slocum sharply as he poured a shot and put down the bottle.

Slocum gulped his whiskey, poured another, and turned slightly so he could see the players and the bar drinkers. He looked casually at the lean-faced gambler. He had high cheekbones, steely grey eyes, a flat black hat and a brown shirt with a shoestring necktie. He looked hard and sinewy. His position at the table let him face the bar, and he played with three big, red-faced cowboys.

Slocum watched for a few moments, heard someone call the lean gambler Hardy, and noted that most of the winnings were piled in front of the middle-aged cowboy whose back was to the bar.

The barkeep mopped the wooden surface of the bar behind Slocum.

Slocum turned toward him and, in a low, casual tone, said, "I'm looking for Dalton, you seen him, mister?"

That jarred the barkeep, and his eyes, dark and shifty, swung quickly to the man called Hardy, then back to Slocum.

"You speaking of Red Dalton?" The barkeep's voice was almost loud. Hardy glanced up, and his steely eyes fixed on Slocum, then he coldly looked back at his cards.

"Yeah, he's the one."

The barkeep kept mopping the wood. "He was here, early afternoon."

Slocum smiled genially. "Where is he at now? Important that I see him."

"I couldn't tell you, mister. He could be back, and he could ride out to other parts. Never know about a man like Red." He stopped mopping. "If you want to leave a message for Red, I'll see that he gets it."

"That right? But you don't know where he's staying."

The barkeep tried to grin, but his black eyes shifted

around a lot. "That, mister, is a great mystery. But people keep meeting up with him. I'd see that he'd get your message."

"You're a good fella," Slocum said with a wicked smile. "Just let me think about it."

He turned to the tables and watched a big pot being played at Hardy's table. Though he seemed to be losing money, Hardy played calmly. His steely eyes moved around the table, and at the showdown, the middle-aged, red-faced cowboy won it. Grinning, he began to reach for the pot.

Hardy spoke coldly. "Don't touch that money, Malone."

Malone stared at him, amazed. "What d'ye mean? I just won it. Three queens."

Hardy stood up. "You won it crooked." His voice was chipped ice.

Malone gaped at him, his mouth open.

"If a man called me crooked, I'd draw," Hardy said, his grey eyes like steel points, his hands at his sides.

Slocum's body was mobilized. The whole play sounded fishy to him, but the hell of it was that he lay in the line of fire.

"Draw, you thieving pig," growled Hardy, and his hand started down. Slocum flung himself flat to the floor as Hardy fired, the bullet tearing the wood of the bar exactly where he'd been standing.

The other players at the card table jumped in front of Hardy, one cowboy knocking the gun from his hand. "You gone loco, Hardy," the cowboy said. "Malone never played a dirty deal in his life."

Slocum dusted his jeans and came toward Hardy. He felt ferocious anger.

"You're mighty careless with that shooting iron, mister," he said.

Hardy stared at him coldly. "Who the hell are you?"

"Let me show you," said Slocum, and he swung his fist with all his force, putting his shoulder into it, at Hardy's jaw. He went to the floor as if he'd been poleaxed. He lay there, stunned.

"Next time we meet," Slocum growled, "try shooting straight." He walked to the bar, stared at the barkeep. "You miserable little weasel, here's the message. Tell your pal Red Dalton that John Slocum is looking for him."

Before he walked out the door, he glanced back. Everyone was looking at him. Hardy, still on the floor, stunned, was shaking his head, as if trying to clear it.

He moved through the door into the street, untied the horse, and started walking. That bastard Dalton had put Hardy up to it; Hardy was one of his boys. It was a clear setup. He'd seen it before: ambush by honest mistake. But the mistake was deadly. In a wide-open town like this one, everything goes.

He stopped at Hawkins' Livery, where the blacksmith, husky and muscular, was firing a horseshoe. He had a broad, pleasant face, alert brown eyes, and looked curiously at Slocum, then at the roan.

"Mighty fine-looking horseflesh," he said.

Slocum looked fondly at the roan. "He's all heart."

The smith smiled benevolently. *He likes men who like horses,* Slocum thought. "Needs fixing the right front shoe."

"Won't take long," the smith said, looking at the hoof. "In town long?"

"Hard to say," Slocum replied.

"Where you from, mister?"

"The name is Slocum. John Slocum. I'm from a lot of places."

"John Slocum?" The smith's eyebrows went up. "Heard of you, Slocum. Didn't you ride with Quantrill?"

Slocum pulled a havana and lit it. He didn't care to think about those days. "Did a lot of riding, and I'm getting tired," he answered.

He watched Hawkins as he worked, pounding the iron on the anvil, his big muscles rippling. "Texas is big country. Plenty of living space here."

Slocum puffed the cigar. "I got a bite of the wanderlust, Hawkins, and just don't know where or when I can put down roots."

"A tumbleweed, eh? That's what happened to a lot of men after the fighting. They just drifted."

Slocum nodded. "Know a man called Red Dalton?"

Hawkins stopped pounding the shoe. "Yeah, people 'round here know him."

"I'm looking for him."

The brown eyes narrowed. "To join him or to fight him?"

"Well," Slocum drawled, "I got a little score I'd like to settle with him. Can't catch up with him. He's slick as a dozen weasels."

The smith nodded. "Dalton's an ornery customer, and it's mighty dangerous to cross him. He's done a lot of killin'. He and his bunch have sure spread plenty of misery through south Texas. I'm thinking good men would breathe easier if Red Dalton got what's coming to him."

"Where does he put himself nights?"

Hawkins rubbed his chin thoughtfully. He was a

discreet man, but a good one. "I heard of you, John Slocum, and what I heard was always good, otherwise I wouldn't be talkin' like this. He has a hideout. The only reason I know is Clem Dalton once asked me to deliver a horse there. Five miles south of Dawson there's a small trail goes sharp right uphill. A cabin, a getaway place. Doesn't mean he's there now. It's all I know."

Slocum looked hard into the smith's brown eyes and put out his hand. "Thanks, Hawkins."

He smiled. "He doesn't operate alone, ever. He's got the bunch—his brothers, Jessie, then the Dakota Kid. All killers. Not here now, doing their mischief somewhere, I reckon."

"I reckon *not*," said Slocum.

The smith turned sharply to look at Slocum, then his broad face broke into a big grin. "If that's what I think it means, that's mighty good news, Slocum. A gun like yours could clean up a dirty town like this."

"Haven't done much with Red Dalton."

Hawkins nodded. "He's the worst." He put the new shoe to the horse's foot and pounded in the nails. Then he straightened up. "There's a cool gun in this town by the name of Hardy. A fast gun. Someone to watch out for. He's a Dalton man."

Slocum's face was hard. "I'll keep an eye for Hardy."

He left the roan and the gelding at the livery and walked into the street under the sundown sky, aflame with bright orange, then started toward the hotel. A call made him stop to look back. A bunch of cowboys were standing on the porch of the saloon, staring at him. Slocum knew the sign; they were expecting entertainment. Then Hardy came down from the porch, threw a grin at the crowd, walked to the center of the street, and, his hands hanging loosely at his sides, started toward Slocum.

The message was unmistakable: showdown!

Slocum thought for a moment about Charity at the hotel, then he, too, moved to the street center and began an easy walk toward Hardy. In the saloon a little while ago he had stripped Hardy, before his friends, of all dignity—insulted him, knocked him down. Hardy was a gunman, and to take it would finish him in Dawson.

So, as Slocum figured it, Hardy told everyone at the bar what he would do to Slocum: shoot his brains out. He couldn't let a stranger, a lowdown hyena, come in and put his dirty hands on him.

That wouldn't have happened, Hardy was thinking, if Red Dalton hadn't insisted on rigging the game so that shooting Slocum would look like an accident. Hardy wanted to take him on straight, insult him, force him to draw and kill him. He'd never been beat in a draw. That damned Slocum had dared swing a fist at him.

He walked the red dirt street, these thoughts running through his head, watching the powerfully built stranger come toward him.

Slocum came, light of step, with intense green eyes, his big hands hanging easy. He looked dangerous, but in his time Hardy had buried a lot of dangerous men.

And Slocum would just be another.

The sun had dipped under the horizon and the sky was burning. A good setting, Hardy thought, for a man like Slocum to die in.

They were fifteen feet from each other.

The green eyes of the stranger bored into him. Hardy could read no fear in that lean, square-jawed face. *But,* he thought, *he'll be dead anyway in the next minute.*

"Slocum." His voice was cool. "You said, the next time we meet, to try and shoot straight. That's what I'm here for. To shoot you straight to hell."

"Try it, Hardy," Slocum said, almost in a gentle voice.

There was the world-stopping pause before the draw, then both moved in a choreography of death.

Hardy's hand streaked to his gun; he was fast as lightning, they always told him that, and now his gun was out of its holster, coming up, he was moving fine, as he always did before the kill, his eye on Slocum's heart. He was fast...

And that was his last thought as Slocum's bullet exploded in his brain.

13

Slocum looked at Hardy. His steely grey eyes were staring still, as if they hated to give up the power to see.

Men came slowly from the saloon and the houses, gazing down at the body with morbid curiosity. Though they spoke softly, their words reached Slocum, who stood frozen, feeling a tightness that came to him sometimes after a showdown.

"Did you see that draw?" whispered one cowboy.

"Never saw it, just heard it," said another.

"Hardy never been beat before."

They looked at Slocum who, for some curious reason, found it hard to move. He was suddenly tired, very tired of killing. He wheeled and started slowly for the hotel. Two days ago, he didn't know Hardy was alive. Now the man lay in the street, dead from a bullet in Slocum's gun.

Did he deserve to die? He'd tried, in the bar, to ambush him, hadn't he? He was part of the Dalton bunch, wasn't he, a pack of vicious killers?

So why this feeling? In this territory you killed to live, and that was that. He never picked Hardy for killing. Hardy had tried instead to knock him out with a phony play about a crooked game. He was rotten. The territory was infested with rotten men, greedy, violent men who used the gun to get what they wanted. Someone had to stand up to them, or they'd take over the land. They used guns, and the only way to stop them was with guns.

He began to feel better. The tight feeling in his gut that came after killing seemed to ease up. Clem and Jessie, the Dakota Kid, Hardy, all vicious men. They spoiled life, so they didn't deserve to live. He was stupid to feel bad about the shootings. Texas was cleaner without them. And the most vicious of them all, Red Dalton, still breathed and did his dirty work. Until Red Dalton was dead, evil in the territory was alive and kicking.

His step was lighter as he walked into the Dawson Hotel. "Miss O'Rourke," Slocum said.

The clerk, a thin, balding man with a big Adam's apple, told him, "Miss O'Rourke is in Room 9." There was respect in his voice.

Slocum went up the stairs and knocked on the door. She opened it, and her flower-fresh young face broke into a big smile. She pulled him into the room and hugged him. He liked the feel of her sweet-smelling body against him. He wondered if she had heard the shooting.

"You smell good," he said.

"A hot soapy bath does wonders. You might try it some day, Mr. Slocum."

"I tried it years ago." Slocum grinned. "Have you had your dinner?"

"Waited for you," she said pertly. "Don't aim to eat a feast by myself."

They walked down the street to the restaurant named Mama Joy's, a clean spacious place with scrubbed oak tables. Mama Joy came out in a calico dress, a bright, smiling woman with curly brown hair, brown eyes, and high cheekbones.

"What'll it be?" she asked cheerfully.

"A hunk of steak, done good, some yams, corn, and peas, and after that a good hunk of pecan pie and coffee. How's that?"

"You've got it, Mr. Slocum. It's real nice to have a man like you in town," she said. "Sort of makes the place more fittin' for the ladies to walk the streets. Clean out the trash, I always say, and this would be a fine place to live." She put her hands on her ample hips. "You made a fine start today, cleaning it up. I'm going to give you the best piece of meat in Texas, broiled real good in onions, and my special sauce. And my pecan pie is the best in the territory, folks say."

"Achin' to try it, Mama Joy," Slocum said. He'd been eating trail meat, and craved home cooking from a talent like Mama Joy.

After she left, Charity said seriously, "I take it you didn't find Red Dalton. You'd have said so."

"He's not in town, but he's not far away either." He felt grim, as he always did when he thought of Red. "You once said Dalton's not running from me.

I think you're right. He's just in a hurry. And just puts other men out to stop me."

"Like Hardy," she said.

His eyes flickered.

"Oh, we heard the gunfire in the street. Word gets around like brushfire. Somebody ran in and told us in the hotel that a stranger called Slocum just shot Hardy, the gambler." She gazed at him. "Why Hardy?"

He shrugged. "One of Dalton's men. They keep coming out of the ground like rattlers."

Her lovely face scowled. "If you shoot the head rattler, Red Dalton, all the snakes will disappear."

He grinned, especially when the steaks came out, great hunks of meat, seared brown and juicy, and yellow corn, green peas, and orange yams.

He was on the pecan pie, looking out the window, blissfully about to enjoy a second bite, when he saw the three riders. They rode tall in the saddle, all big, bulky, powerful men in big hats and frock coats, and each wearing two guns. The grim, broad-faced rider in the center with the murderous look in his eye was Sean O'Rourke. The other two men, whom he recognized as big time Marshal town-tamers, weren't smiling either. They rode past the restaurant, their eyes straight, clearly headed for O'Toole's Saloon.

Slocum didn't waste a minute. He gulped down the piece of pie already in his mouth, pulled some money from his pocket, dropped it on the table, and grabbed Charity's hand.

"What is it?" she scowled, hating to be interrupted in her enjoyment.

He turned her loose. "You can stay and meet your dad if you want." When he reached the door, he peered to the other end of town, where the riders, guns out were pushing into O'Toole's Saloon. Slocum moved into the street with Charity on his heels, and went fast into the livery where he'd left the horses. The smith looked up astonished as Slocum slapped money into his fist.

"Thanks, Hawkins, and goodbye."

They swung over their saddles and put the horses into a quick pace, moving out to the red dirt of the street, then to a gallop.

At the end of town, Slocum threw a look over his shoulder. O'Rourke and his men were still in the saloon. He raced toward a shelter of trees, thinking he had all the headway he needed. The roan and gelding would stay out in front.

He would work his way south, toward Dalton's hideout.

Things seemed to be closing in.

His wide swing in a great circle brought him to the south trail. He slowed the run. O'Rourke, Steele, and Barry were riding powerful black stallions, so there was good reason to believe they were not far behind. O'Rourke had his first real smell of the quarry, and he didn't intend to slow down. The look on his face stuck in Slocum's mind. He looked ready for murderous games. He had suffered not only the loss of his daughter's purity, but the two ranch hands, Caine and Lowshot, killed brutally, which O'Rourke would know, for he was the kind of man to dig up the graves. And the riders with him, Barry and Steele, were slim-hipped, broad-shouldered men, deadly with guns. They had tamed a couple of bad towns in the Arizona Territory. O'Rourke could afford to hire the best.

Slocum was not interested in hanging around and

sparring with such men. He had no quarrel with them; all he wanted was Red Dalton.

The trouble was Charity. He liked her, enjoyed her, and she was beautiful on the bedroll, but he had a man's work ahead of him, and she lay on his neck like a ball and chain. There were tricks he could do, turns, backtracking. He could use all the trail cunning he'd learned, but most of it was out because of her.

It would be smart to drop her at this crucial time. He needed time to work Dalton alone. Might even slow up O'Rourke, to get his daughter back in good shape. Maybe he would drop his crude idea about avenging himself on Slocum.

These thoughts streaked through Slocum's mind, then he sighed heavily. She was no longer the sweet young innocent O'Rourke fondly remembered. She'd barreled into the world of love, and O'Rourke was not going to congratulate him for that.

Also, he had to remember that she'd helped him shake loose from Caine and Lowshot, and he owed her for that. It wouldn't be easy to detach her from this showdown. She'd come to get Dalton. Why should she go now, when the showdown seemed so near?

But he should try.

They rode on, and when they reached high ground, even though the light was fading fast, he climbed the rocks and looked back at the trail.

There they were, the three small figures, what was left of the posse, riding the trail straight for them. In fifteen minutes, it would be dark, and they'd have to stop for the night.

He, too, would pitch camp, but not before he got to striking distance of the Dalton hideout.

They rode in the darkening gloom, and by the time they reached the cutoff on the side of the road leading to Dalton's cabin, a quarter-moon was out. Enough light to shoot by, but not enough to track by.

He would bed down about fifty yards off, in a shelter of trees and rocks, good defense ground, if needed.

When they settled in their bedrolls, after he had taken care of the horses, he looked toward her. She'd been strangely silent, even remote. In the moonlight, her face always took on a mysterious glow, which he sometimes noticed in beautiful women.

"What's troubling you, Charity?" he asked.

"Why'd you say that?"

He smiled. "You're not your usual bubbling, babbling self. Is it because your dad is near?"

She sighed. "I got a bad feeling."

"What kind of bad feeling?"

"Dunno. It looks like roundup time, one way or the other. Either we get Dalton or he gets us. And Dad is here to push things to a rough end. I know him. He's hard."

"Those men with him, Steele and Barry, they're hard, too; town-tamers. I've heard of their work in the Arizona Territory."

Her blue eyes looked dark and strange in the gleam of the moon. "So, Slocum, this could be our last night."

"Could be."

She stared at him.

"Aren't you goin' to do anything about it?"

He grinned. "I'd like to do plenty, but I can't help feeling uneasy, with your dad breathing hell and brimstone about a mile away."

She glared. "Are you going to worry about him at this late date?"

"Yes."

She scowled. "That's cowardly."

"Yes."

A pause. "Listen, he's bunked down for the night. We can't worry about him," she said.

"Well, beautiful young thing, it's not easy to romance you, with everything out there, and lots on my mind."

Her brow lowered, and she looked heavily displeased. "Must say a woman wouldn't describe you as the perfect lover."

"Not hardly," he said. After a pause, he went on, "If you were a wicked woman, I suppose you could start a fire that a man couldn't put out."

"What do you mean?" she demanded. "Are you saying that an experienced woman could do wicked things to men, and they couldn't help themselves?"

"Yep."

She looked thoughtful, lay back on her bedroll, and seemed to meditate on the moon.

He put his hands behind his head and let his body relax, thinking that, come tomorrow, he'd need to keep his wits sharp.

He watched the quarter-moon, low in the sky, start its upward climb, looked at the willow above him, its leaves hanging dark green, like a painting in the dead air.

Nature was silent. Even the insects were still, as if, after a busy, buzzing day of eating and being eaten, everything in nature wanted rest.

Charity squirmed in her bedroll, something working in her mind.

He decided then to make his pitch. "Charity, I've been thinking we could avoid a lot of grief if you were to go back to your dad tonight."

She didn't move, just lay quietly, then came up on her elbow, her eyes glowing in the moonlight. She said nothing, just stared.

"There might be a lot of shooting tomorrow," he went on. "I wouldn't want you to catch hell. When bullets fly, people get torn to pieces."

"I can't believe my ears," she said. "After all we've gone through to get here, you're telling me to run back to Daddy."

He cleared his throat. "It's not only for your sake, Charity. This is man's work. I got to be honest. You cramp my style. I have to think of you, every step I make. It gives Red Dalton the edge."

She leaned toward him. "Since I've been with you, you beat the Comanches, Dakota, Hardy. Did it in spite of me. How?"

"Mighta been easier if I didn't have to think about you."

She glared. "Let's go over this again. Caine and Lowshot had you roped up like a steer, ready to deliver you to Dad. I saved your hide."

He felt himself shrinking a bit. It was damned true. He might be singing like a soprano now if she hadn't pulled Lowshot's gun.

"I don't deny it. I'm beholden to you. But we got a tough situation now. I have to think about Dalton, and also those men with your father. They're tough, dead shots."

"So you're afraid," she said scornfully.

"I'm calculating the odds," he said fretfully. "If you go to your dad, you could talk to him. It would give me time. I don't even know if Dalton is *in* that cabin."

Her eyes flashed. "You want me to tell him you're all right, that you don't deserve to get castrated?"

He had to laugh. "I don't deserve that. Think of the fun you would have missed."

Her anger faded for the moment. "You deserve a gold medal for that. But I've told him all that. And he told me to shut up. That I was a ruined girl. That he was going to make your punishment fit the crime."

Slocum scowled. The single-minded idea of O'Rourke was cause for serious concern. And with those two deadly town-tamers to help him, there was a lot to worry about. That was what he meant, telling her she was a grievous load on his mind.

But even if she went back to O'Rourke, it wouldn't melt down that iron man. He wanted revenge. And, damn him, it was hard to tell if he wanted his revenge more on Dalton, who was the real skunk in all this. He himself was just an innocent tool in this game.

Charity had been watching him. She spoke up firmly. "I came to get Red Dalton, and I'm sticking to the bitter end. And that, cowboy, is final."

Slocum looked up at the sky, now punctured with billions of glittering diamonds. That was that. He'd made an honest effort. She'd be safer with her father, and he, too, would be safer if she were out of this thing.

But father and daughter were cut from the same stubborn cloth, set on getting their way even if the skies fell.

His conscience, anyway, was clear. He had tried.

"All right, Charity. We're in this together, to the end. For better or worse."

"Like marriage," she said brightly.

"Oh, shut up," he said. "Get some sleep. We got a big day coming."

14

He heard her movements, but it seemed part of a dream, for he was thinking of what strategy to use in his approach to Dalton's cabin, and how to keep out of the clutch of the posse.

The images in his mind began to twist and distort as if he'd eaten loco weed, and suddenly he was holding up his hands, because Steele and Barry had the draw on him, and O'Rourke, with a fiendish grin, had a branding iron, and was bringing it to Slocum's crotch.

And the thought raced through his head, that he'd rather be dead, so he made a break, but they pinned his arms, and he was in the clutch of freezing fear, as the scalding iron was brought closer and closer, and it was so hot it was cold, and with crazed effort he got free, grabbed at the iron, and to his amazement found himself holding Charity's hand. She was bent low over his jeans, her mouth pressed down. She glanced at him, and noticing his eyes open, said, "You told me a wicked woman would know how to persuade a man to make love. I think I know what you meant."

She brought out his organ which, because of the fear in his dream, lay limp and listless.

But the sight of Charity so near and the touch of her lips brought on the miracle of maleness, a rising from the dead, and it stood up, proud and pulsating. This seemed to do powerful things to Charity, for she bent to kiss it, to rub her lips against it. The movement of her mouth did further miracles, wiping out his will power and all further thoughts about strategy against Dalton.

She moved her mouth on him, then stopped and looked at him.

"Well," she said.

"Don't stop."

A gleam came to her eyes. "Is this what the wicked woman does to make the man make love?"

He inhaled deeply. "You're a quick learner." He pulled off his clothes, then pulled hers off.

"Now," he said, "what were you doing?"

"Something like this," she said, and her mouth went back over it. Her skill amazed him. He felt a great surge of passion but he fought for control, turned her on her back, nibbling at her nipples, stroking her body, going down over her body, and put his lips to her, and soon she was moaning in what sounded like agony.

Then he went between her thighs, thrusting all the way, his bigness filling her. She moaned with the pleasure of it.

He grabbed her body and began to plunge repeatedly and she groaned, and every so often he'd pause to put his lips on her breasts. Her arms were tight as a vise about him, as if she wanted to merge her body into his.

He held hard to her buttocks and kept plunging deeply into her, and she had her legs thrown about him, coming up to meet his rhythms, her body pulling on him, and in a trance of pleasure they continued on and on, until finally he felt the coming, soaring climax, and his body held on a peak of unbearable tension, then he exploded. In some mysterious way, it set off her release, too, for she made a strangled sound, as if in pain, then went limp under him.

Then he heard the voice, and his heart nearly stopped.

"That was a pleasure to watch, Slocum."

It was Red Dalton's voice, with a heavy sneer.

He stepped from behind the thick brush, his gun pointing. He was grinning ear to ear.

Slocum's gun in its holster was just an arm's length away, and his eye flickered to it.

"Go ahead, Slocum, reach for it," Red mocked, his dirty yellow-brown eyes shining in the moonlight. "Go ahead, I won't kill you. Just bust your arm."

Slocum froze.

Red studied him, then Charity, whose gunbelt also lay within reach.

"I'll shoot you, too, little lady, just as quick as I'd shoot him. No difference to me." There was something in the flat, dead tone that made them believe him. He was a killer, and killing a woman didn't matter to him.

They lay there, their bodies sweating from love,

and now as near to death as the whisper of a wrong move.

Dalton came forward, stepping light, astonishing in so big a man, his gun cocked. He moved quickly, took Slocum's gun, stuck it in his belt, and flung Charity's gun far back in the bushes.

He stared at Charity's body, and his tongue ran over his lips. "Never would believe you were a virgin so recent, little Charity. Mr. Slocum shore put a lot of ideas in your head. I got a few things to teach you, too. By the time we're through you're gonna be good as a first-class whore."

His broad, blunt, red-bearded features twisted with a cruel smile. Then his tone hardened. "You see, Tad Dalton gave up his balls for you, so I figure you owe the Daltons an awful lot."

He turned to Slocum, his face fixed in a look of malevolent hatred. "As for you, Slocum, I don't know if I can ever figger out the best way to pay you off for what you done to the Daltons. But, believe me, I got a lotta good ideas. Shootin' you is the last thing. You ain't goin' easy, Slocum, you're goin' in the worst way. But I'll let you try to imagine how, while we ride. Now get dressed, both of you. Don't forget, I won't hesitate to shoot, but the shootin' will break your bones, make you bleed, but I'll keep you alive."

Slocum put his clothes on, and while he did, he cursed himself. He'd been soft-headed and let his good sense get lassoed by a pretty girl. He'd let his desires run wild here, within a quarter of a mile of his quarry, when he should have been all tuned up. He'd been screwing when he should have been scouting. And this was the bitter payoff. It was the girl; she'd seduced him with her body, and it had put him under Dalton's heel. He drew a breath. He was at fault himself, of course. He could have forced her off, ordered her to go back to her father, he could even have ridden off from her. He was at fault.

Was this to be the end?

Dalton was clever; he knew what he was doing. He'd come down noiselessly, from wherever, to nail them. It took trail knowhow.

He felt cold fury at himself and at Dalton. The slimy hyena had stayed in the brush, and watched the lovemaking. There was no limit to his evil. And who knew what he had in mind for the girl.

But as long as Slocum had life, he had hope.

They mounted up, and Dalton led the way, Charity following, Slocum last, in a single file. When they stretched out a bit, Slocum thought that he might twist the roan off at the right moment and try a getaway.

Dalton, as if he read the thought, turned and reined up. His grin was hideous. "If you try to run, Slocum, I'll shoot the roan. And you'd just have to ride double with the girl. So don't get ideas."

Charity spoke for the first time. "You're so low-down, Dalton, you'd shoot a horse."

"I'd do much worse than that, pretty girl, to keep Slocum with us. But don't fret, honey. You and I'll have some fun."

"Fun! You pig! I wouldn't want to be in your shoes when my father catches up with you."

He glowered. "O'Rourke is one gent I want to keep alive. Just so he learns what has happened to the apple of his eye, his darlin' Charity, the cutest gal in Texas. I want him to remember what he did to my kid brother Tad. Now ride."

They rode through brush country, and, to Slocum's

astonishment, not to the cabin, but farther south, through timber country.

The trail became convoluted, and for some time Red's face scowled a lot, as if he might have drifted from his destination.

But they came finally to a log cabin cloistered in a bunch of pines, surrounded by soft earth, and a grin spread over Red's bristly face.

"There it is, just where it's s'posed to be. What d'ye think of that, Slocum?" He didn't wait for an answer. "Well, this is a good place, with a lot of nice surprises in it. I'm goin' to show it to you." His mouth hardened. "I got a special feelin' about you, Slocum. You did me such a lot of misery, I don't think, if you lived ten lives, there'd be time enough to wipe it out."

He put the horses behind the cabin, and with his gun out, brought them to the door. It creaked loudly as he forced it open.

It smelled musty, but the air cleared when Red pushed open the small front window. It was spacious, with an iron cooking stove, cooking utensils, four cans over the stove. There was a wooden bed with a beat-up red blanket, a wooden locker under it. In the center of the room were a table and two roughly built chairs.

Red pointed to the bed. "Sit there, both of you, and don't move unless I tell you."

Then he cut some rope and gave it to Charity. "Tie his wrists real tight." He held the gun on them. Charity tied the ropes, and Dalton checked them, then growled at her to tighten them more.

He started to search the room, opening the cans, the cupboards, the footlocker. Each time he came off empty he cursed under his breath. He gazed around the room, frustrated, saw a loose board on the floor, pounced on it, pulled it up, but found a bottle of whiskey. In disgust, he almost flung the bottle at the wall, thought better of it, opened it, and took a long swig.

"Can't find the money, eh, Dalton?" said Slocum.

Dalton glared at him. "What the hell do you know about it?"

"A lot of people know you busted the bank at Fort Worth."

Red scowled, then grinned. "Yeah, we did it, the Dalton bunch, busted the bank at Fort Worth. Devlan and that bitch, Maude, ran the money into this place. That's what he tol' me before I shot his damned head off. Maybe he was lying. But he couldn't be. It's gotta be here." Suddenly he stopped and stared at Slocum. "You shot my brother, Clem, didn't you? Then Jessie, then Jody, Dakota, Hardy." A doleful look passed over his face, and he took a long drink, wiped his mouth, and stared at Slocum. "You wiped out the Dalton bunch, Slocum, you rotten bastard." He swung his fist. Slocum turned his face fast, but the blow still stunned him.

"You'll pay, Slocum, you'll pay. But all in good time. There's a lotta fun in you two. Don't wanna kill the fun and games, do I? Red Dalton's a lotta things, but stupid he ain't."

He wandered the room again, going over the same ground, emptying the pockets of the clothes in the footlocker, going through the boots, searching the cans and every crack.

He found nothing, and his eyes turned sullen, his mouth mean.

"That scum Devlan told me with his dying breath the money was here, and I believed him. But he went to hell with a lie in his mouth." He grunted like a pig. "If only I had his rotten hide now." He glared at Slocum. "But I got you here." He took another slug. "I could beat you to a pulp. That'll come later. Maybe I'll stud you with her again and watch it." He grinned fiendishly. "Damned good fun watching you two. You like the little filly, don't you? I'll tie you up real good later and let you watch her and me. You'll get a kick outa that." He mopped his mouth with his sleeve, his eyes fixing with riveting intensity on Slocum.

"Lemme tell you what I got in mind for you after. Gonna nail you to the ground where there's some good fire-eating red ants. Gonna plug your eyes open so you get plenty of sun, and let the hungry ants do their dirty work." His face shone diabolically. "I thought of every which way to kill you, Slocum, and decided that was the best. And I'll stick around, you know, come back every hour to see how you're gettin' on. Soon you won't be able to see me. You'll be stone blind. And you'll be yellin', yellin' your rotten brains out as the ants eat you alive."

He looked at Slocum, waiting for a response, his face grim. "Not bad, is it? But you'll have a lot of time to think about all the Daltons you shot. You broke the Dalton bunch, Slocum, and you're gonna die the worst kind of death there is.

"Meanwhile, I'll be amusing myself with your lovin' gal. She sure got to be mighty interestin', in the ways of love she's learned from you."

Dalton's face twisted with an evil grin as he stood nearby.

Slocum glanced at Charity; her face had gone white with horror. She couldn't imagine a man like Red Dalton. Slocum feared for her, what she might say, and anyway, he felt he had nothing to lose. In fact, it might be better to force an end.

As if stiff and wanting to loosen up, he stood and stretched, then bent, then with a sudden spring to the right, he butted his head low into Dalton's gut. It knocked Dalton back and he fell. His eyes seemed to start from his head, his face paled, but his hand still clutched the gun, and, though he was in agony, he started to bring it up to fire. But Charity flung herself at his hand, pushing it, and the bullet hit the floor.

It was all Slocum needed. He went out the door like a shot, sprinted to the heavy brush. He heard the scrambling, wrestling, and cursing inside the house, and raced farther into the brush, looking desperately for a hiding place. He needed time.

But that was not to be.

"Just stand right still, and I won't blow your brains out," said a calm Texas drawl. Slocum looked into Marshal Barry's light brown eyes, his strong-jawed face, his big Colt pointing right at Slocum's head. Slocum cursed his luck. He recognized the marshal who had tamed a couple of bad towns in the Arizona territory, a big name in the West. Then Barry did something Slocum never dreamed would happen. He raised his head, curiously, to look at the cabin.

A gun barked and a red hole burst in Barry's forehead, and he dropped like an empty sack of potatoes.

Slocum, already bent low, flung himself flat to the ground and crawled behind Barry's body. Alive just moments ago, he was now totally dead, but his fingers were still warm as Slocum prodded the gun from his hand. Slocum couldn't help feeling a surge of relief as he held the gun in his tied hands, and he peered at the cabin for Red, who'd made a fantastic shot, considering all he'd drunk. The moon, unfortunately, threw down plenty of light.

Red was peering from the door. He had to know now that O'Rourke was nearby, that Slocum, with his hands tied, was lurking in the brush. He wanted, above all, to get a shot into Slocum to keep him grounded.

For Slocum, the main thing was to keep Red in that cabin until he could untie his hands. He sighted along the barrel, holding the gun with his tightly tied hands, then fired. Red jumped back and a string of curses came from the cabin as Dalton realized Slocum now had a gun.

His heart beating hard, Slocum bent, pulled his knife from its hiding place, and, holding the knife between his knees, slit the ropes. He moved his arms to circulate the blood, then bent to pick up Barry's gunbelt.

Somewhere nearby, prowling, had been three men, and they had come at the cabin from different directions, and Slocum had stumbled into Barry. That damned fool had underestimated Red Dalton and caught a slug in his head. A sad, quick end. Marshal Barry might tame a town, but he forgot for a second the first law of survival: stay under cover. Dalton, peering from the cabin for Slocum, instead saw Barry, and with lightning speed took him out.

Dalton had always known he was trailed by Slocum, and that both were trailed by O'Rourke. He made no great effort to lose his pursuers; he was never going to put himself too far from Slocum and the girl, Charity. He had played a cunning game about the money cabin, holding back until he could trap Slocum and the girl. He always knew where they were, and when they started their love games, it gave him his chance. Up to now, Red had figured Slocum was one of the deadliest men he'd ever met. He had singlehandedly mowed down his gang, some of the fastest guns in Texas. It had been a bitter thing for him to learn that, one by one, his men had been gunned down. Slocum had to be either amazingly lucky or the smartest cowboy he ever met. Then Slocum made the stupid mistake, screwing the girl just outside Red's hideout. That did it. There was no way a man could screw and protect himself at the same time. Even a man like Slocum.

When Slocum scrambled out of the cabin, he had a shot at him, but that cursed filly deflected his aim. It took him a full minute to subdue that wildcat, and only a hard right to her jaw did it.

Now Dalton had to figure the angles. There were three men outside his cabin, but they were not only hunting him; two of them hunted the third. Dalton scratched his groin. O'Rourke wanted Slocum as much as he wanted him.

When he figured everything, Dalton felt he had the odds because he had the girl.

His grin was evil.

15

Slocum studied the land around the cabin: pine trees, thick brush, some rocks, and soft earth. Plenty of places to work from. Most of all he wanted to get to that cabin now that he had a gun. O'Rourke and Marshal Steele wanted that, too, but they also wanted him. What would O'Rourke do, he wondered? Go for him or for his daughter?

Then he heard the whisper of a soft voice. "Barry?"

Not O'Rourke. It was Marshal Steele wanting to find out who had caught the bullet from the cabin.

Slocum slipped deeper behind the boulder. "Steele," he said softly.

A long silence while Steele digested the idea that his sidekick had got it.

Slocum spoke again. "Dalton got Barry, shot him from the doorway after I made a break."

Steele did some thinking, then he sounded skeptical. "Makes a good story, Slocum. Why not shoot you? Why Barry?"

"He's saving me for a Comanche-style death. Red ants. I'm not his favorite."

"You're not O'Rourke's, either." Silence. Then Steele spoke again. "So Barry got it?"

"Yep."

Silence.

"All right. Give yourself up. I'll get you a fair trial," Steele said.

"For what?" Slocum asked.

"For violating a charity."

Slocum laughed. "You're a funny man, Steele. I'd get strung up before trial."

"Might be better than a branding iron on your balls."

"Look, Steele, in case you don't know, Dalton forced me with a gun."

A long pause. "All right, I believe it. Tell it to the judge."

"Steele, I got no time for morons. Dalton's got the girl. And it's our job to get her and get him, too. Are you working with me or against me?"

"I'm working for O'Rourke. It's his money. He wants you, Slocum."

"So you won't work with me?"

"Come on out. I don't want to have to go against you."

Slocum shook his head in disgust, but decided, for Charity's sake, to make one more pitch. "Dalton's got Charity. He's the lowest kind of polecat. He'll stop at nothing. Tell O'Rourke I'd like to help him save the girl."

Steele spoke slowly. "O'Rourke thinks she's in there because of you. If she hadn't followed you, she wouldn't be there. It's all because of you, Slocum. You're his number one. So you're mine."

They're both a couple of brainless fools, Slocum thought. Then his ear picked up a soft sound. So, all this time Steele was talking, O'Rourke was trying to move behind him. Another boulder lay ten feet away, to the left of Steele's position; it would protect him from O'Rourke, but might expose him to Steele. He had to move toward it or attack O'Rourke.

He crouched low, almost to his belly, and squirmed forward, leaving the protection of the boulder. Steele fired at his movement, and Slocum, from his new position, fired back; the bullet surprised Steele, and he shifted sharply, which suddenly left him partly exposed; he cursed and tried to scramble back, but it was too late. The gun barked from the cabin, the bullet tore the side of his scalp, and Steele plummeted back.

The silence was deadly.

Slocum felt the sweat on his lip and wiped it.

He had a bad feeling about Steele.

If he was gone, then there would be only O'Rourke left, and he didn't seem to care what happened to his daughter.

He crawled to Steele's position, and found him on his back, the blood from his head saturating the grass. He had a handsome, rugged face, with bright blue eyes that stared empty at the night sky. Slocum gazed at his bulky body, then took his gun. It was hellish: two town-tamers, the marshals Barry and Steele, famed for cleaning up some of the sinkholes in the territory of Arizona, wiped out in minutes because they didn't know every moment in the wild was a killing moment if you didn't stay covered.

He crawled low behind the boulder, listened for sound, heard nothing, and began to think.

Should he try to reach O'Rourke? Reason with him? He felt it would be a losing battle. The man was a hard-head; it'd be useless. He'd probably think Slocum had finished off his marshals.

He peered at the cabin. Should he try for it? Was there a way? Dalton was a deadeye, never missed, and didn't seem to let his mind wander. He was a survivor and, Slocum felt, one of the most dangerous men he'd faced. How could he get into that cabin? How get Charity away from that rotten skunk?

Dalton, he knew, wanted him to try, yearned for him to try. He'd never be happy until he paid off the man who had killed his kin, until he paid him off like the Comanches did with their most hated enemies.

Slocum's position at this boulder was not the best. O'Rourke knew he was here, and so did Dalton. He had to move. Staying flat, he crawled slowly, and at no time was he a target for gunfire. He moved to another boulder fifteen feet away.

What now? The longer he waited, the worse it could be for Charity. Dalton was drinking, and if he felt there was a standoff, he would use the time to amuse himself with the girl. He might be doing it now.

The moon, damn it, gave too much light. Dalton could shoot either from the window or the slit in the door. He had cover in the cabin, though there was a blind side to the right, and he had the girl. Slocum's trouble was he didn't know what O'Rourke was thinking. What did he want first: his daughter or Slocum?

He felt tired. It had been a long, long day. He lay behind the boulder where he could smell the coarse earth, the fresh pines, the night breeze scented with summer flowers. The chirp of crickets filled the air, and he looked up at the dark blue sky with its brightly silvered quarter-moon. A beautiful night, not for killing but for loving. And two marshals lay dead just twenty feet nearby. Before the sun came up, he wondered who else would be dead, never to see another beautiful night like this.

He took a deep breath and in every inch of his body felt the pleasure of being alive. Hoping that after sunup he'd still be alive. But the odds were not with him but with Dalton. Because he had the fort which had to be stormed, he had the girl who had to be released. How to do it? How? If he made one mistake, two guns would hit him, O'Rourke's and Dalton's. He couldn't afford one bad step, not even a bad half-step. He studied the ground and tried to think out O'Rourke's position. He was big, not young, but a man of experience, and would not take chances.

In that case, he'd be farther back, maybe on that rising slope. What the hell was he going to do? Time was passing.

"Dalton. Red Dalton." O'Rourke's deep, harsh voice bellowed. It came from the high ground.

There was a long silence.

"Dalton. This is O'Rourke."

"I know who it is."

"You got my girl there."

"Yeah, I got her."

"Turn her loose, and I'll put five thousand dollars in gold at that door."

There was a long silence. Then Dalton's voice. "But she ain't worth that much any more, O'Rourke."

O'Rourke's voice went hoarse with rage. "Just turn her loose. I'll make it ten thousand."

"She's just a tramp now, O'Rourke, not worth a dime."

The silence was horrible.

Slocum could feel the blood in his temple begin to pump. And he could also feel the suffering of O'Rourke. He began to move silently.

"Dalton, you never had a daughter. You don't know what a father feels."

"I know what a brother feels, O'Rourke. You hurt Tad in the worst way."

Silence.

"But the girl is innocent." O'Rourke's voice was broken. "She did nothing. Why hurt her?"

"I don't want to hurt her, O'Rourke. It's you I want to hurt. *She's how to do it.*"

"I'll give you fifteen thousand, Dalton. Turn the child loose."

The size of the reward, Slocum reckoned, must have made a big impression on Dalton. He was silent for a time. Slocum stopped crawling until they talked again. He was trying to get to the blind side of the house. He was thinking of something.

Then he heard Dalton, as if he'd been considering O'Rourke's offer. "All right, fifteen. Where's Slocum?"

"Slocum? Who the hell knows? If I knew I'd blast him to hell."

"Well, Slocum is part of this deal. If I get the money, how do I know Slocum will let me walk away?"

"Kill the bastard," O'Rourke snarled. "Then you can walk away."

"Saying it is easy. No deal. This is the deal. Slocum brings the money."

"Are you crazy?"

"That's the deal, O'Rourke. Slocum brings the money. He comes to the door. Leaves his guns."

O'Rourke swore. "How the hell am I gonna get him to do that, you moron?"

"Temper, Mr. O'Rourke. We can have a deal. Just talk to Slocum. Slocum will do it. He can do anything. Ask him."

After a silence: "I'll talk to him. The money's on my horse; it'll take time to get it."

"Go get it and talk to Slocum. I got plenty of time. I got the girl."

Silence fell on the night.

O'Rourke's voice. "Slocum?" His voice was polite.

"Yeah?"

"Did you hear Dalton?"

"I heard him."

"Let's talk. I suggest a truce. I want Charity more than I want your hide."

"I'll come to you. Just wait."

Slocum examined the ground. About forty feet to the left of the cabin, the earth was soft. He could work there, if he was quiet and quick. It was the blind side of the cabin. Dalton would never know what was happening. Not unless he opened the door. If he did that, Slocum could shoot.

It was not a bad bet; one worth taking.

He needed one thing from his saddlebag, and the roan was behind the house. This was his one advantage. Though Dalton had Charity, he was locked in, but Slocum had the freedom to move, and that meant something.

Working flat on the ground, he finally reached O'Rourke. The big man glared at him, but said nothing.

"I'll take care of it, O'Rourke," he said in a low voice.

O'Rourke's broad face glowered. He hated Slocum's guts, but he was feeling like a father. "Get my girl away from that rotten dog, Slocum. You owe me that. She wouldn't be there if you didn't start it all."

"Everyone played a hand, O'Rourke. What you did to Tad started it."

"Hell, *he* started it. Tried to rape Charity."

"So Dalton wanted to pay you off. And *me* for shooting Seth Dalton in Abilene."

O'Rourke's head hung. "I want my little girl, Slocum. He wants your skin. I know you cleaned out the Daltons. He's not gonna let you live."

"Get the money. Take your time. I'll meet you back here."

He watched O'Rourke leave for his horse, thought hard a few minutes about what to do, then started for the roan. There wasn't much time to daybreak, and the moon still shone brightly.

Dalton grinned as he drank from the whiskey bottle. He had them over a barrel. He had the ace card— Charity. And O'Rourke would give his eyeteeth to get the girl. And Slocum, some kind of a hero and idiot, would offer himself. He was stupid that way. He played on the side of the angels. There were men like that in the world, who thought your job, while you were alive, was to be good. It was nonsense. He'd learned early, you took what you wanted if you had the gun, and the weak ones who played straight took the crap.

He'd take the money from Slocum, shoot his brains out right off. He had no time now to fool around with the red ants. He'd take the girl, too. If O'Rourke tried to get in the way, he'd blast him to hell.

He liked the girl, liked the things she did with Slocum. She'd do them with him, too. He thought of her curvy body, the way she used her mouth, and it made him drool. He'd wait, though. He was no damned idiot like Slocum who, because he let his head get muddled with sex, was going to pay with his blood.

He gulped booze and looked at Charity. "You shore got a lot of good looks, honey, and we're goin' to have a lot of fun. I was hopin' to find the bank money here, but your dad's goin' to give us some."

"Aren't you goin' to let me go?" she demanded.

"Shore, shore," he said, and grinned. "But first we're goin' to have a lot of fun and games, me and you."

Then he heard Slocum's voice. "Dalton."

He went to the window, but could see nothing. "Yeah?"

"The money's near the front door."

"No, it isn't."

"It's there. Take a look."

"Where the hell are you?"

"Back, way back."

"You sound mighty close."

"Voice carries, the wind. Look out the window; you won't see me."

It was true, Dalton could see nothing. And he

couldn't see the money. He was furious. He had expected Slocum to bring the money. "Where's the money?"

"It's at the door. I told you," Slocum called. "Let the girl out."

"You son of a bitch. You're supposed to bring the money and your guns. We don't have a deal."

"I'm not an idiot, Dalton. Now, I've left you the money, done my part. I'm leaving. Do yours. Let the girl go."

"You busted the deal, Slocum. The girl goes with me. Hostage, till I get clear of both of you. One wrong move, she gets the bullet. Move back. I'm gonna check if the money's there."

"I'm nowhere out there. Look for yourself."

Dalton peered out the window cautiously on both sides. It was true. Nothing in sight, nothing nearby. Not a sound, not a whisper. He felt safe. He unlocked the door. Now he would open it just a crack, pull in the money. Then he'd have the girl, keep her in front of him and get away.

He cracked the door, gun in hand, and slid to the floor and crawled forward. He could see the bag of gold just five feet from the door. He could reach out his hand to pull it in. Again he looked around everywhere. Nothing. He crawled out, grinning ear to ear, then his senses shrieked with alarm, but he could see nothing, didn't know where to fire.

The ground moved. A pair of eyes, a hand came up out of the soft earth, a gun belched, and the moment he knew, he knew nothing as the bullet plunged through his right eye, blasting out the back of his skull.

Slocum came up from the hole in the soft earth forty feet on the blind side of the cabin that he had dug with his shovel, quietly and quickly, burying himself, shovel, and gun. Only a space had been left for his mouth. His position was impossible to see from the cabin unless Dalton opened the door. Coming out of the earth was a Comanche trick. He had seen it once and remembered it.

He dusted off the dirt from his face, his hair, his clothes, walked to the door, pulled Dalton's body aside, and stepped into the cabin. Charity was lying on the bed, her wrists and legs tied. Her eyes gleamed with joy at sight of him. He reached for his knife and slashed the ropes.

She threw her arms around him as O'Rourke came in the door.

He stared at Dalton, then at Charity, and pulled his gun. "All right, Slocum. I owe you for what you did to Dalton. But I still owe you for what you did to my little girl. Throw your gun."

Charity glared at him. "Are you crazy, Dad? He saved my life!"

"Shut up. He still did the wrong thing to you. Throw your gun. I'm taking you in."

Slocum threw his gun on the bed.

"All right, move toward the door," O'Rourke said grimly.

Charity picked up Slocum's gun. "Don't move, Dad."

He glared. "My own flesh and blood! You're forcing me to kill him!"

She pulled the trigger, and O'Rourke jerked his hand as if he had touched a hot stove, dropping his gun. She reached down for the gun she'd shot from his hand.

"You just don't know when you're ahead, Dad."

Slocum came over, took his gun, and grinned at her. "You're a dead shot, honey. I think you got a few things to teach your dad. And some growin' up to do."

He paused, let his eye travel around the room. "By the way, there's one place Dalton didn't look for the bank money. I just wonder."

He walked to the stove and lifted the stove top, stared into it, then reached down for the three bags of gold inside, pulling them out.

He fixed his eye on O'Rourke. "I'll leave them with you."

He reached for Charity and kissed her. "I'll come back and look you up some day. You'll be a woman then. Goodbye."

She took a deep breath and with tearful eyes watched the lean, rugged man walk out as the sky turned to dawn pink.

It looked to be a beautiful day.

GREAT WESTERN YARNS FROM ONE OF THE
BEST-SELLING WRITERS IN THE FIELD TODAY

JAKE
LOGAN

JAKE LOGAN

___	0-867-21087	**SLOCUM'S REVENGE**	$1.95
___	07296-3	**THE JACKSON HOLE TROUBLE**	$2.50
___	07182-0	**SLOCUM AND THE CATTLE QUEEN**	$2.75
___	06413-1	**SLOCUM GETS EVEN**	$2.50
___	06744-0	**SLOCUM AND THE LOST DUTCHMAN MINE**	$2.50
___	07018-2	**BANDIT GOLD**	$2.50
___	06846-3	**GUNS OF THE SOUTH PASS**	$2.50
___	07046-8	**SLOCUM AND THE HATCHET MEN**	$2.50
___	07258-4	**DALLAS MADAM**	$2.50
___	07139-1	**SOUTH OF THE BORDER**	$2.50
___	07460-9	**SLOCUM'S CRIME**	$2.50
___	07567-2	**SLOCUM'S PRIDE**	$2.50
___	07382-3	**SLOCUM AND THE GUN-RUNNERS**	$2.50
___	07494-3	**SLOCUM'S WINNING HAND**	$2.50
___	07493-5	**SLOCUM IN DEADWOOD**	$2.50

Prices may be slightly higher in Canada.

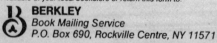